UNBLOCKED

The Blocked Side of Facebook

Anonymous

Author: Anonymous
Country: US
Language: English
Publisher: WRITE it PUBLISH it, LLC
Publication date: 2012
Media type: Print
Pages: 232
ISBN-10: 0985771607
ISBN-13: 978-0-9857716-0-7

Disclaimer

Contents

Introduction

Facebook has become a daily part of life for people these days, especially teenagers. It's a way of communicating through the web and showing who they are and what they do. Teen's post what they think, eat, say, feel, and every other little detail that happens to them daily. Basically, most teenagers share their entire life over Facebook. In Unblocked you will see what teens are going through, how they talk and feel. The reader will be entertained by the raw emotion, rage, joy, laughter, and out of control fights, on every page. Trust me when I say you will not be able to put this book down.

Preface

The purpose of publishing this book is simple: entertainment and awareness. Awareness of what type of things may be posted on Facebook. This book will show readers the interesting things that can go on in a teen's life on Facebook.

Although this book will make your jaw drop at times, it was not written to offend or upset anyone. Some posts are funny, some not so, some crazy, some sad, and some eye-popping. It will make you laugh and sometimes, even cry. Just be a fly on the wall and watch as these crazy stories unfold before your eyes. You will get to know the characters; love them, hate them, pity them and at times, admire them.

I hope people who read this book see there is both a right way and a wrong way to use this powerful media tool. I also have faith that most will see the power it can have to cause pain and joy in a person's life and take great care and use compassion. When used for the right reasons, Facebook can truly be a connection to the other people in your life and bring us all together a little better.

WORST FACEBOOK FIGHT

Stacey	**The most fucked up thing that anyone has ever done to me, and I didnt yell or name call, I just put it behind me. Soo i guess this is growing upp.**
Bojie	**best thing to do fuck all the bullshit**
Althea	**is it what i think ur talking about??**
Stacey	**kynsley and robb fucked and she told me about it and i just said if you apologize were fine. and she did so its whatever.**
Althea	**:(i know and im sorry that that happened to u girl.**
Stacey	**its fine :) anything that doesnt kill you makes you stronger. so i just gotta get myself up and move on with my lifee hahah**
Althea	**aww your taking this so well and being so mature my little Stacey is growing up :]**
Stacey	**ahaahah awh i knoww huh :) thank you aha!**
Daniel	**Your confusing**
Stacey	**i got over it, then i didnt**

Stacey	**chill slut.**
Rocky	**is this status to like every girl in town?**
Stacey	**no one in peticular Shella**
Rocky	**woahhh here comes a fb fight im excited**
Kynsley	**this is dumb. delete this shti.**
Rocky	**here we go....**
Shella	**eww, immature, you're one to talk.a hahahahah**
Rocky	**ROASTED!**
Stacey	**SHELLA DONT EVEN GO THERE Ive been with one guy, you dont even know how many youve been with stfu**
Shella	**ahahahahha. SIKE. you may have given your virginity to one guy but your mouth has been around the town.**
Kynsley	**oh my god ^**

Chad	:)
Rocky	ahahahahahhaah
Stacey	your vagina has been around the town bruhh, its the easiest catch in town once you through alcohol in you
Andrea	im only commenting on this so i get notifications when you guys commment back to each other ahahah sorrrry im really bored right now
Stacey	ahahahahahh Andrea
Shella	throw*....you're boyfriend cheated on you. BAHAHHAHA.
Kynsley	oh fuck.
Stacey	i wasnt going out with him awk ahah, and the guy your in lovee with fucked everyone THEN you, sooo you =0
Rocky	damn and it only gets better as the fight goes on!!!
Chad	Stacey 3-0 Other chick 0-3
Stacey	:) i trryyy bruh ahaha
Shella	in love with? bahahahhaha. bullshit. the guy you're in love with left a tramp stamp on your bestfriends neck.
Chad	ahah im entertained :)
Kynsley	oh my fucking god, i'm outt, late.
Rocky	your not out its just getting good!
Kynsley	definatley about to get bitched at for the rest of eternity
Stacey	who am i in love with aha? if i wanted to be with robb id be with him, you couldnt be with david if you BEGGGED HIM, which you already pretty much did. and whos neck? are you fucking insane, he didnt even hook up with marilyn ahha. get yourr shit striaght if your trying to "hurt my feeelings" coz its not really getting to me with you false statements.
Rocky	MOATED!!!!
Shella	ahahahahhaha., deff not talking about marilyn right now, and btw they really did hook up. and i want nothing to do with david, this is what i mean by you think you know all my shit when you don't. ahahha, get a clue.
Shella	the reason robb won't hang out with you = his neck.
Fabian	anybody wanna sandwhich?
Rocky	ahahah we got some grumpy people... grumpy people are hungry people get them all sandwhiches (:

Stacey	ahah well care to share with me slut? And robb's been begging to hangout with me and ive been busy ahah, you want EVERYTHING to do with david, even after he fucks all your friendds. you get a condom! you are such a fucking whoree ahhaah
Kynsley	did not want this shit to come out this way.
Rocky	i do... its fun
Andrea	fuccck i really need to sleep but i'll wait until this is over hahahhaha wtf is wronnng with me, i have no lifee ahhaha
Stacey	what are you talking about, text me back
Rocky	noooo no texting stay on comments!!!
Shella	i don't wanna share shit with you, not trying to get that disease. and maybe he found some makeup..kynsley's neck is a different story. you are soo wrong about david, especially since i'm not even friends with him on fb and shit. you think you're fucking in my life? like you have no social life with anyone at our school anymore, don't try to act like you know shit still, you don't.
Fabian	guys, listen to yourselves. im not gonna get involved, but i will say this. youre freshman right? its HIGHSCHOOL dude. in 3 months you will be bestfriends because you realize youre both working off misinterpretations
Kynsley	okay, i really fucked up & i'm sorry, but i'm not dealing with this drama.
Fabian	just take a step back, is this REALLY worth all the slander?
Stacey	fuck that be a fuckign real person and own up to your shit
Kynsley	theres no need for an explanation, so drop it. late.
Rocky	ohhhh here we go again after a lil break to get all theyre hair back its round two!!
Rocky	its hella worth the slander
Shella	iiight i'm not trying to be in this pussy drama. deal with your shit yourself Stacey, and don't act like you know my life. you're not in it anymore so don't bother.
Stacey	Im over you Shella your just a whore and it annnoys me. so why the fuck is kynsley being such a sketchy slut and fucking my ex
Rocky	OHHH SHITT!!!!ROASTED!

Rocky	**kynsley you better hop in this shit entertain me!**
Stacey	**OR PRIVATLY TEXT ME BACK**
Shella	**if you're saying i'm a whore, own up to your shit too. ahahahha nbd, you didn't wanna be with him anyways ^^^^**
Stacey	**i didnt shes just a shitty person, she deserves everything jess puts her through.**
Rocky	**FUCK THAT NO TEXTING THATS NOT ALLOWED!**
Kynsley	**i let go of jess , thanks. you know that saying "to get over someone, get under someone else" , sorry.**
Shella	**ahahahahh, obvi he was on topp ♥ noooo big deal homes. you get what you deserve.**
Rocky	**ohhhhhhhhh shit!!!!!! kynsley 1**
Shella	**you don't want him, and the alcohol she consumed that night did, soooo.....shit worked out.**
Dingdong	**hahahaha i love facebook fights!:D**
Kynsley	**no, her boy just wasn't in check like he was supposed to be.**
Rocky	**oh damn keep that pimp hand strong!!**
Stacey	**Shella go talk to someone whos willng to get close enough to you to catch all your deiseses coz im pretty much over your aids an bullsshittt.**
Shella	**homie hopper, you'd have the same ones.**
Dingdong	**you girls should really eat chocolate, i heard it solves everything!:D**
Stacey	**Kynsley who the fuck are you shut the fuck up? yu werent in check either, your fuking stupid. Shella you FUCK EVERYONE like i cant comprehend how loose your vagina is and how low your morals are, SHUT THE FUCK UPP AHAHAH**
Rocky	**both of you got moated just on that one...damn**
Dingdong	**my vagina is pretty loose too, SOOO WHAT!**
Andrea	**hooowww sad))):**
Stacey	**yeah my life sucks**
Shella	**ahaham, it might solve everything, but it won't get rid of Stacey's stds and anger management....my morals might be low, but at least i still have them thizzhead. ahhaha, yeahh my vagina is really fucking loooose. NOT, bitch. stop talking your shit, you don't know anything.**

Dingdong	well look on the brightside of things you guys made my night:D
Shella	ahahaha, slut alerttt
Cheyenne	SLUT SLUT SLUT SLUT SLUT SLUT SLUT SLUT SLUT SLUT SLUT SLUT SLUT SLUT SLUT SLUT SLUT SLUT SLUT SLUT SLUT SLUT SLUT SLUT SLUT SLUT i'd rather have a hickey than an std like this bitch ahahahaahahhaahahhahahaa Stacey you're sexy i love u
Rocky	your life sucks compared to what?
Stacey	SHELLA go die of aidss alreadyyy, and youve thizzed jsut as mnny times as i have ahah? i love you Cheyenne :) oh soo much
Rocky	way for dirty drugs like ecstacy!!!!!
Rocky	YAY*
Dingdong	smoke weed kids.......
Rocky	fry face kids (:
Shella	ahahahahah sike, who are you trying to impress right now? no one gives a fuck, you're mia from the world anyways.
Rocky	boom!
Dingdong	i like turtles....
Kynsley	booooo
Cheyenne	oh drugs yummy. (; i love u too ahahah this is the best chick fight of my lifee.
Dingdong	ewwyyyyyyy
Stacey	i wish i could say youy went mia froom the world but you just hop from dick to dick contracting a new deises each time :(
Dingdong	mmmmmmmmmmmmm dick
Rocky	LAWLING
Kynsley	i seriously think i'm on punked right now, ashton you can come whenever you want ya know?
Cheyenne	hey Stacey, its funny how your MIA, when im pretty sure the whole world just saw you last night at that party? that was probably the dumbest thing ive ever heard in my life.
Shella	disease************** get your shit right, it's bugging me. ahaha, you're a joke, i'm over your pathetic low life.
Andrea	i'm not gonnna be able to wake up tomorrrow, so goooodnight everyonee ♥ loveee you guyyys! (: hahaha
Jan	this is interesting :) hahahah.

Stacey	ahhahhahaah i love being MIA IN the midst of a on of people that actually matter not consisting of stupid sluts who would only be aloud in the door if she gave the guy head ahahah. its buggging you i dgaf :)
Dingdong	everyone should just stop for a second.......and think. WHAT WOULD JESUS DO?
Stacey	jesus would tell Shella shes a whore, hes embarassed he created her
Kynsley	gods making us do this right now, if you really think about it.
Dingdong	haha^ prolly the stupidest thing ive ever heard.
Rocky	im glad he is he must have known how bored we are
Kynsley	Ahahahah if sierra was here, we would totally explain to you fuckers how god is making us have this fight right now.
Calvin	ew this is so immature.... Stacey just fight a bitch. :)
Rocky	keep it up on here then if there is a fight someone post it on fb
Calvin	I would just delete this posting & then block her. :) you win.
Cheyenne	time to fuck a bitch up Stacey. beter get on that(;
Calvin	^ ratty #2 ohh wait you guys are friends...awk.
Shella	alright immaturity has kicked to a whole new level and i'm fed up with this bullshit. you may think you know what you're talking about, but you fucking don't. ahahha. gtfo, and learn to spell, THAT'S ALSO PISSING ME OFF. Stacey doesn't catch fade. Ahahah
Calvin	^^^ your soo cutee ı)
Kynsley	who are you ^
Shella	uhmm awk...this kid is talking to whooo....?
Cheyenne	HAHAHAHAHAHA def very awk. ahahahaha oh well fuck it.
Calvin	^^^ ♥ freshies. (; Hey Cheyenneee lets pull another krista...
Cheyenne	UHHHHHMMM pretty sure he's speaking to you? the arrows were pointing to your comment. ahahaha dumb bitch
Kynsley	*sophomore.
Shella	over this, i'm out. ♥ ♥ ♥ ♥ ♥
Calvin	that makes you sooo much cooler :)
Cheyenne	wow big difference. besides, he wasnt talking to you.
Cheyenne	krista #2, next weekend. im on it baby boo.
Calvin	na na na hey hey goooddbye, I love Stacey and i've never met her yayy. :) hellaaa gonna go get a dozen x 20

Kynsley	let me guees? you fucked up krista?
Calvin	hahaha no Kynsley
Calvin	butttt just shh from now on.
Jan	notice how Stacey hasn't said anything for the past like 5 minutes. hahahaha. okay this is none of my business but it's funny :) k byeee love you allll.
Calvin	thanksss :
Rocky	Stacey backed out
Cheyenne	Stacey 's amazzzinngnggg ♥ lets just get the wholeee entire section this timee
Cheyenne	& nah, didnt fuck up krista at all, i like her.
Calvin	shee hass long hair and doesn't care. :) I just want her to feel sepcial when she gets back on here and sees notif x 200. Naw she probably went to sleep. this is all bull shit.
Kynsley	ssh from now on ? hayhayhay your the one that popped out of nowhere budddaye, and awwe love youu jan! ♥.
Cheyenne	& i did notice that, but if you think about it, its probably cuz she logged off (;
Calvin	well crazy sierra wont kill usss (: ♥
Kynsley	she's still signed on?
Calvin	kynsley you kinda look like a dog.
Dingdong	why dont we all just have a fat brawl? RAGE!!!!!!!!!!!!!
Stacey	BACK BITCHES
Shella	okay all of you can gtfo so i stop geting notifications, thanks.
Kynsley	thaaaanks ♥ is that supposed to bother me? ahaha.
Calvin	just delete yourself from stacey's life^^ thanks :(
Calvin	Are you still talking? adalfjaflasjfl fml.
Cheyenne	a fugly motherfucking dog.
Stacey	Shella i tried kicking you ass previously and your cheerleader ass ran for the hillls so fuck you! hop offff mine and the males of our towns dick, we dont need anymore stds spred through the world. no guy wants filth. bye byee slut :) fin with you
Cheyenne	STACEY GET UR ASS BACK ON (:
Calvin	rufff (:
Calvin	id fuck her, she sounds easy.
Stacey	i love calvin, Cheyenne, and jan juss sayinn!
Kynsley	ew what the fuck bitch ^ tryna catch fade or what ?

Shella	ahahahha. heard ass ♥ someone's grown upp.
Calvin	heard ass? Who was just talking about spelling? awk...
Shella	hard ******** awk, myyyy bad.
Calvin	good night every one, sweet dreams :).
Cheyenne	you got a lot of nerve saying that shit when your bitch ass is sayin just as much shit. step the fuck up & say it to Stacey's face. scared or what?! HAAAA BITCHHHHHHHHHHHHH
Kynsley	i don't even fucking know you, jump off my genetials. and last time i asked Stacey to catch fade she backed down, get your shit straight , me and Stacey have already talked, i'm not fucking in this shit, so calm your tits. LATE,
Shella	sweet dreams to you tooo :) i can't say it to the bitchs face since she's so damn mia. bahahha. suck my dick and let the cum melt in your mouth.
Jan	"I wish we could all get along like we used to in middle school. I wish that I could bake a cake made out of rainbows and smiles and and we'd all eat and be happy."
Cheyenne	then get the fuck off & stop writing shit.
Shella	bitch who are you even talking to ?
Kynsley	HAHAHAHHAHAHAHAHAHAHAHAHAH AHA JAN I JUST DIED.
Shella	agreed. jan oh jan. P
Dingdong	Stacey and Kynsley should fight jus sayinnnn............
Calvin	Why areyyou guys saying fade, your all little white bitches that live in this town. god damn.
Cheyenne	Stacey should fight Shella & Kynsley, jus sayinnnnn....
Shella	you guys should all gtfo because Kynsley's already asked Stacey to catch fade and she backed down.
Nikki	This conversation just kept me very intertained.(:
Cheyenne	HHAHAHAHAHAHAHAHAHAHAHAHAH AHA
Dingdong	dammmm Stacey is a crazzyyyy bitch! fightin 2 bitchess n shit DAYYUUMMMM!
Calvin	Shella don't talk like that....your like a five year old cheerleader.
Shella	ahahhaa. pretty sure i'm fucking older than Stacey....who you're defending?
Kynsley	Dingdong , me and Stacey don't have a problem, awkward.

Cheyenne	than why dont you step up & do somethin?
Dingdong	how bout we just say were all in mma an call us "professional fighters" an act like were hard?
Kynsley	alright let's.
Dingdong	naww that was a joike tehe
Shella	where's Stacey, that's the bitch i have a problem with, not all of you guy. get off my genitals
Kynsley	well everyones acting like there hard and popping up out of nowhere, so might as wellllllllll
Chad	I like real women.
Cheyenne	nobodys on your genitals, your're a dirty skank. trust me, no one wants to be up on that shit. so stfu & dont say that. k thanks.
Calvin	wait, you guys realize Stacey doesn't have to say anything? Backkfaddeeee<---yeah im a gggg.
Shella	aahahahah because you fucking know me right? i'm not dirty skank, so you're not welcome
Kynsley	Shella's not how Stacey ortrays her too be, beeeetuubs.
Cheyenne	from what ive heard, you get around... therefore your a dirty skank (:
Calvin	Stacey is a friend obvis gonna stand up for her? dadjadajdADasdada just go smoke a bowl and hit the sackkk
Kynsley	does this girl even know you Shella?
Dingdong	hell yeah smokke weeeed nigggga!
Stacey	dgaf about kynsley, TRIED FIGHTING SHELLA, AND WOULD HAVE KILLED HER IF SHE HADNT RAN AWAY AND TOLD OUR SCIENCE TEACHER TO MOVE ME ACROSS THE CLASSSROOM. calvin and Cheyenne are amazing and im covered in sluts, tthank god i dont goo to that high school.
Calvin	I just keep hearing barking fm l
Shella	from what you've heard? ahahah, bitch, stop listening to what you hear, its all shit talk. NO THIS BITCH DOESN'T KNOW ME; SO SHE SHOULD GET OUT.
Calvin	waiitt stacey where do you go
Dingdong	wheres waldo?

Calvin	Shella this isn't your wall so you should hop of Stacey's nuts. So Shella text me, im dtf.
Shella	ahahah, yeah you so would of dominated? that's why you ran to the fucking office and tried getting me kicked off cheer? reall sly boobear.
Dingdong	yeah im dtf toooo i like being sluttty
Cheyenne	I DONT NEED TO KNOW YOU, ALL I KNOW IS YOUR A DUMB FUCKIN CUNT & YOU NEED TO SHUT UR FUCKIN MOUTH
Calvin	I love stacey I love stacey I love stacey I love stacey I love stacey I love stacey I love stacey I love stacey I love stacey I love stacey I love stacey I love stacey I love stacey I love stacey I love stacey I love stacey I love stacey stacey I love...
Calvin	I love stacey I love stacey I love stacey I love stacey I love stacey I love stacey I love stacey I love stacey I love stacey I love stacey I love stacey I love stacey I love stacey I love stacey I love stacey I love stacey I love stacey stacey I love...
Calvin	I love Cheyenne. I love Cheyenne. I love Cheyenne. I love Cheyenne. I love Cheyenne. I love Cheyenne. I love Cheyenne. I love Cheyenne. I love Cheyenne. I love Cheyenne. I love Cheyenne. I love Cheyenne. I love Cheyenne. I love Cheyenne. I love Cheyenne. I love Cheyenne. ...
Dingdong	i like being slutty i like being slutty i like being slutty i like being sluttyi like being slutty i like being slutty i like being slutty i like being sluttyi like being slutty i like being slutty i like being slutty i like being sluttyi l...
Calvin	so much love in the air
Kynsley	yes Shella, you're a dirty cunt, but i love you so it's okay :)
Calvin	kynsley some one has too?
Stacey	Shella your an ignorant whore, dont talk to her like that, she has respect and you have none so you have no right to act like your higher than her. i tried ruining your life and almost succeeeded dfumbcunt :L)
Cheyenne	& this is why i love you so much calvin ahahahaha
Stacey	I LOVE CALVIN I LOVE CALVIN I LOVE CALVIN

Calvin	Stacey just unfriend herr and we can talk shit on this and she cannt see any of it.
Jan	am i the only one who loves everyone ? ...awkkkk.
Jan	hahahahaha
Calvin	Cheyenne im calling you b
Shella	not trying to be in your immature drama anymore. grow the fuck up and stop trying to put other people down because you're life sucks, you tried ruining my life? but didn't? what a fail, sorry to hear that.
Cheyenne	hahahaha i seriously dont have any respect for her. Stacey, you tried.. it didnt work out.. lets try again (; bitch better WATCH OUTTTTTTT
Dingdong	dammm thats fucked up^
Kynsley	funnaye, how Shella's on the phone with me dying becuase she can't catch her breathe from laughing so hard..........
Dingdong	ferreal do
Calvin	damn 211 comments. Stacey your famous :)
Shella	ahahahhahahahhahahahhahaha hhahahahhahahaHahah h ahahhahahahahhahahahahahha, MY LIFE IS AWESOME.
Calvin	not even.
Kynsley	mliaaaaaaaa.
Cheyenne	your life can suck a fat dick,
Dingdong	my life is sluttttyyyyyyy!!!!!!!!!!!!! !!!! wooooohoooo!
Calvin	d
Calvin	a
Calvin	a
Calvin	asf
Shella	according to Stacey, my life doesn't suck a fat dick, i do. but i'm not sure what pill she's on right now
Calvin	dfgh
Calvin	sdf
Calvin	sdgh
Calvin	sgh
Calvin	dfas
Calvin	df
Calvin	dfas
Calvin	g

Calvin	**fgh**
Calvin	**dfas**
Calvin	**fsd**
Calvin	**gfd**
Stacey	**Shella your life sucks, you will die of aids at 25, alone because no one wants a loose pussy, bye. :)**
Kynsley	**can someone delete this guy already? ^**
Shella	**agreed kynsley.**
Calvin	**Im just gonna blow up your notifications till you guys get offfff Stacey's wall**
Cheyenne	**can somebody just slit ur wrists already, cool.**
Shella	**i'm not on her walll, i'm on her status.**
Stacey	**SHELLA IM ON VICODINE DUH, OMGOMGMOG ALWAYS ON PILLSS. Sike**
Stacey	**pilllspillssspillsssspillss ss yuumyuymyu**
Shella	**i wouldn't be surprised. ahahhaha**
Cheyenne	**whats wrong with pills? i take them 24/7.**
Shella	**which is why you're all crackwhores who have no lives.**
Calvin	**crackkkwhoree baby**
Stacey	**i have to be on pills to deal with your anooying ass, you invite yourself to my house and i tell you to sit outside**
Cheyenne	**curb stomp.**
Niño	**you guys are crazy!**
Shella	**ahahahahhahahhha. sike, you're "best friend" hits me up so she's not bored and we leave you alone at your house..**
Dingdong	**fuckk yeahhh ladders all dayy nigga!**
Dingdong	**yum yum yu**
Cheyenne	**she wasnt alone, she had me. SO SUCK IT**
Shella	**pretty sure you weren't there. Ahahhahahah**
Nikki	**Agreed Niño.**
Dingdong	**I'm rickk jamess bitch!**
Calvin	**Omg does this bitch have a mute button?**
Cheyenne	**pretty sure i wouldnt go till ur nasty ass left /:**
Kynsley	**my sister really did come to get us tho.**
Stacey	**you left because i was yelling at you to shut the fuck up every second, and p.s your "best friend" was telling me you invted youself over and she didnt want you to come either sooooo.**

	your annying. dont open your mouth unless your sucking some dick coz its alll your good at Shella
Shella	ahahahhahahahahhaahah. fuck sorry i contaminated the house mannn.
Calvin	Stacey please please please delete this :
Cheyenne	gag.
Stacey	but i love it ahahah :)
Calvin	omg Stacey you almost got 300 comments.
Dingdong	were sooooo coooool
Stacey	ahah i know bitches have alot to say i guess
Shella	ahhhaha, at least i'm good at somethinggg homie. and i'm pretty sure we both left your sick ass at home to go kick it with other people. ahhahahahhaha. whatevs.
Stacey	and sluts have even more to say... ahah
Cheyenne	they only have a lot to say over the computer. HAHAHAHA
Shella	sike...ahahha, bitch hasn't even met me before.
Calvin	haha ohh yeah lets see how far cheerleading takes you? nooo where..... Try getting a scholarship for that. it wont hold plus they don't accept sluts to college
Kynsley	wtf, i wasn't even aware of the situation, i just woke up bros, coool stories tho, tell them again please,but this time leave me out of it.
Cheyenne	definitely dont even wanna meet you but aight.
Calvin	Wait isn't it past all our bed times?
Stacey	hahha so you left me sic you think that reallly upsets me because it doesnt, it just shows your a shitty person. and im glad its shinning through. im happy david fucked the world then gave you the stds, i really am :))
Cheyenne	not ours... but theirs, yes. oh youngsters. how cute.
Stacey	i dont count coz i dont have school mondays :)
Calvin	whyyyy?
Stacey	what>
Cheyenne	UHHHHHHHHHHHHMMMMMMMMMMMMM M
Kynsley	bithces be crazy these dayss....
Stacey	sh
Shella	i'm bored with this....your bullshit doesn't interest me anymore

13

Calvin	then why are you posting holy shit!
Kynsley	Jan i fucking love you, jusaayin.
Cheyenne	Shella your a slut, go away.
Stacey	Shella can you leave so we can talk shit on you
Shella	Jan, i deff love you also ♥
Calvin	Wait hang on, whose Shella?
Stacey	no one loves a hoe Shella
Cheyenne	UHM i dont know, ive never heard of her? Ahahaha
Shella	are you gay? for real?
Stacey	i have, from numorous dicks
Calvin	(:
Stacey	id rather be gay than flamming hoeoeee
Calvin	For you Shella.
Shella	ahah, i'm deff not gay, obvi since Stacey's saying i suck all this dick and shit
Calvin	do they realize were all laughing bout them?awkkk
Cheyenne	she probs goes both ways. HOEEEEEEE
Calvin	iiii go both wayysss
Jan	bahhahahahhahaha i'm just sitting here liking everyone's comment. but i love you allllll ♥
Calvin	I dontt knoww u
Shella	this didn't get me anywhere. ahahha. soo i'm out ♥
Calvin	You keep saying that...
Stacey	Shella you dont suck as much dick as yu ride
Cheyenne	you've said u were out at least 20 times.
Kynsley	pro's and cons about this facebook fights, pro- kept me entertained since i'm not sleepy, con- me and Shella have to get up in 4 hours, to get ready to go get cofffeee, booo at least its with her, :) love her! gooodnight guys, love you allllll :)
Calvin	no one cares about your life....
Stacey	bye kynsley.
Stacey	AHAHAHAAHAHAHAHAHAHAHAHAHA HA
Jan	hi, i'm jan :)
Stacey	HI Jan :) youve liked all my comments and i avent said hiiiii !
Calvin	NIPPLE
Stacey	TITTAAYYS

Jan	i know Stacey, suchhh a bitch move, but hi :) you're famouss, i love you omgg♥
Calvin	ess over. I'm done. 344 comments Stacey ur famous.
Cheyenne	i worship you Stacey.
Stacey	ahah i truelly am a bitch ohh well :/ , ahah thanks guyss. i love you Jan omgg♥yaya calvin, i worship you Cheyenne, im giving you a crown
Stacey	i wanna go read all this again kinda haha
Calvin	i couldn't
Cheyenne	ahahahah okay ill get u a tiara :p
Stacey	Cheyenne i did beauty pagents i have some we can wear mwuahhaha. and i couldnt either calvin its too muccchh
Cheyenne	oh yay time to play dress up ♥
Calvin	hahaha Cheyenne used to be a balerrreniaa
Cheyenne	leotards& tutus, lovely.♥
Stacey	Cheyenne has the cutest pictures in her rooom ahahha :) YOU WERE A BALLERENIAA HAHA
Calvin	yess thats it!
Calvin	hahaha Cheyenne can we finish ur newww room!
Cheyenne	hahahaha both of u shushhhhhhh
Calvin	no
Stacey	i love you both alot p.s
Lucas	don't know one person in this shit but Stacey definetly won hahah
Stacey	yay :) AGREED, Shella has a lung disese though so i think shes gona die before 30...awk
Stacey	ahah thanks bruhhh :) and fersuree, always stayyin upp
Clinton	Dingdong told me to read the whole fight... Not happening..
Tope	hahaha yeah he told me too, im to lazy though.
Tryna	Go Stacey !!! ♥ Cheyenne Calvin ♥
Tope	love you too Tryna ♥
Andy	i tried to read all of this.....waaay too much.
Stacey	I LOVE TRYNA
Tope	my names not calvin);
Tryna	thanks i love you tooo GIRL !
Tryna	I MMEAN TOPE FUCK I FUCKING LOVE YOU TOPE <33333333

Tope	woww! you really called me calvin dickk!! hahaha but i love youuu ♥
Lysander	By far the best facebook fight ive everrrrr read :) thanks guyss <33
Fabian	i love how many times everyone said "eff this im out" then came back.. haha
Theresa	Tiffany told me to read this............and I just read every comment, I ovbiously have no life but I love you Stacey!♥. Hahahaha this was entertaining :)
Lysander	you'reee def not alone theresa! ahahaha guess who HASNT been doing anything else but this? aklsfhklsah how saddd.
Stacey	ahahahah i have no life for being involoved. i love you to theresa :)
Theresa	Ahaha I've seriously been sitting here since 4:18 reading all of these comments! And yes I agree by far the best facebook fight.
Stacey	ahah thanks girl! i just hope you dont think im horrible now aah, its just i find out she fuckedmy boy of a year it blewww aha
Theresa	:) Hahaha but the thing is, no one told anyone to comment it? So she kinda brought it upon herself... but alright!
Theresa	Oh and I don't think you're a horrible person, its understandable.. I have no respect for people who don't have respect for themselves and can go around and do anything with someone that their "friend" was with
Stacey	ahhahaha yess exsactlyyy hahha i freakkin luhh you aha!
Theresa	Doesnt*hahaha :) the feeling is mutual!
Bliss	i HIGHLY agree with Lucas! hahaha. you girls are insane. and yes Stacey def roasted these dumb bitches hahaha♥
Stacey	ahahahahahhha hate it, we are insannee :/ and yay! i lovee youu ahhah!
Lucas	Hahaaha too many ppl are liking that comment.
Stacey	what comment Lucas?
Lucas	You can message me haha. And the first one I put Stacey haha
Lucas	Aw bliss why'd you delete " message me Lucas" hahahah fake ppl these days
Hilda	wooooow, the other one was bettter! Stacey wtf.....lame :

Stacey	**ahah i loved this one!**
Hilda	**ahaha, this one is kinda funny**
Stacey	**ahhaah its less vish ahah**
Rylie	**Well, fuck, tell us how your really feel. haha!**
Stacey	**What**

Stacey	**Telling offf your best friend fucking, ex-boyfriend, at 3:40 im the morning because your a fearless bastard like me :)**

Stacey	**the moment when everyones creeping on your facebook fights and writing status's about it hahaaaaaaa.**

Felix	**awk...**
Natalie	**facebook creeping is my life.♥**
Stacey	**id say**
Tope	**(;**
Fidel	**Everyone in this town haha**
Stacey	**MLIA**
Lysander	**this shit is just too good to ignoreeee Stacey hahahahahhah**
Miriam	**just about to make this my statttus. Awk**
Julia	**well putting it on facebook preety much expands it for everyone to see..if you guys wanted to keep this fight private you would be fighting in person and definatly not on facebook?**
Julia	**so ofcaurse people are gonna say things..**
Stacey	**ahah yeah i know this whole facebook bullshit was dumb!**

FACEBOOK FIGHTS

Kynsley	you're so fake, like slut shut up. bahahaha, :) i love daniel & malou.
Daniel	:P
Kynsley	(: hi
Daniel	Hello;))
Stacey	Awwww I love how you say you wanna hangout with your "bestfriend" ..when two seconds later I was "fake and a slut" your just mad cause I'm hanging out with them and not you.
Kynsley	oh really, i'm oh so mad, actually i'm not, i definatley feel sorry for them cause you with your diaherrea of the fucking mouth has talked shit on each and every single one of them, and yet the funny thing is your such a bullshitter you think they'll never find out, your pathetic. getout.
Daniel	Ooh shit
Joan	^^^ lmao
Daniel	Hahaha joan
Stacey	Considering you texted me three times cause I didn't text you back...I would think you were a little mad...And honestly... Your a dumbass...these people actually don't let middle school drama.. As in, "talking shit on each and every one of them... WHEN I DIDN'T KNOW HALF OF THEM" like wtf? You just sound dumb. Get over yourself... Stop trying to be hard. You straight up asked me to hangout today and cause I was with them, you fucking do this. Hey, your true colors show... I know who my true friends are. Bitch.
Kynsley	thanks for the novel. I definatley texted you once after you K'd me saying "your so fake bahahahha bye" malou was even there, so here we go again with your little lies, witch isn't a surprise since you lie about everything like the faact that you hooked up with stephen the same night you broke up with your bf, who was in the hospital OH and dont forget john the

guy you did shit in front of everyone with (; yuuumskeeezy mc SKEEZ, you definatley thought dave was too much of a "bad influence" on you, you thought mariel was a crazy druggie, & you thought rose was "annoying". you don't even know the definition of friend bahaha but okay huutch :)

Kj   im the real slut here:(

Stacey   Go slit your wrist. Your used to it.

Raymond   damn calm down yuhguyz are friendz yuh dont need to be fukin arguin over stupid shit evan tho i have no clue whaa yuhguyz are arguin bout i still kno itz stupid!!!!!!!!!

Kj   that was bad!

Kynsley   oooh, harsh. because that's such a big deal right ? i'd rather have problems of my own, then be a fucking slut and have everyone know about it. hah, Stacey you do your own thing, and get the fuck off my status.

Stacey   And I definatly heard about the dicks you've been sucking, "you fuckignskeez" and yeah you told him you'd break up with jess for himm? Hmm, good luck ever getting back with him. Ohh wait it wouldn't matter anyways considering he doesn't wannt youuuu :) byee

Kynsley   Mhmmm, i don't want jess Stacey :) but that was a goood one, anyways i just wanted to get my point through how DIRTY, you truly are. but it's cute how your making up these lies, ♥

Stacey   Ahhaa deny away boo, you always do :) Wonder why all your old friends are ditching you and shiit? Its coz you're too much fucking work, you act like we're your boyfrieend or some shit, when I can't hangout you flip ten bitches ahah. You're a fucking mess, keep popping you're exstacy and snorting you're liness, ahah later don't fucking reply

Kynsley   Ahah the fact that you posted on facebook for everyone to see that i cut my self, makes you look worse then i could ever look, because who in their right mind would do that? oh and i'm a mess, oh yeah a big mess because i fucking cut myself, shut the fuck up, you made your self look heartless, and i feel sorry for you sweetie, not me :) byee.

Raymond   Stacey that is soooooooooo fucced up!!!!thatz not evan funny stop putting each otheres buisness out!!!!!!

Kynsley	you should expect it, coming from her ^
Sharmaine	Stacey you're a fucking bitch. its funny how you have to put down other people to make you feel better about yourself. there is no reason at all for you to be putting Kynsley's personal shit up on face book. you're a fucking heart less bitch. Kynsley has enough respect for you to not put your shit on blast. so please do us all a favor and GROW THE FUCK UP.
Tori	Kj's SO right. you guys were friends 6 hours agoo and not only are you guys announcing bad things you did... but Stacey's explaining Kynsley's personal problems to the whole enitre fucking world. this status should be deleted ferreaaaaal. I have no prob with either of you, but this shit is FUCKED UP.
Stacey	For one, check your shit. Your precious Kynsley posted my whole life story on this little status just cause I didn't hang out with her. Therefore, she likes to put down other people to make herself feel better. Fuck off
Kynsley	your whole life story is hooking up with two guys and being a slut, that's definatley something you should be proud of right? i could say so many things about you, but i'll keep it to myself, because i think you've already said enough.
Sharmaine	nawh dont tell me to fuck off. she never once said anything about your personal life. NOT ONCE. yea she called you out for being a FAKE bitch because you're now "best friends" with the girls you talked shit on. im pretty sure anyone would do the same damn thing.
Stacey	Kynsley, stop trying to make youreself look like the victim I wanted no drama with you, I was always the one to text you and make sure you were okay and all this shit, I was there through everything, and you had to hit me where it hurts. So you cant be mad when I gave you a taste of your own medicene. I never intended on hurting you more or using your past against you, but look at this status, you started it.
Kynsley	GET THE FUCK OUT, can you understand that? you made your self look this way, don't come at me with this "your making your self look like the victim" you knew what you were getting your self into the moment your pressed "comment" and i'm fucking done with you, so get off the status, like bye.

Stacey	Ahhaah bye Kynsley, you're fucking dumb. Latee, you know what maybe I am a fucking bitch ahah but at least I have the decency to confront you instead of posting "indirect status'" which you claim to hate soo much. Byeeeeeee crazy bitch
Kynsley	has anyone noticed like how bi polar she is? bahahaha, sorry jusaayin`. no we all know your a bitch Stacey, you can leave now, and oh big whoooop my first indirect status, i called you fake, OH SHIT. i called you fake on a text message straight to your number too stop being all keyboard happy. laate.
Stacey	You're annoyying as fuck! Bye aha
Kynsley	you keep coming back to this status? what the fuck ? bahahahahhahhaha, can you comprehend what i'm saying, ? YOU CAN FUCKING STOP .
Nikki	Awee. Kynsley its all good chick . And your friends didnt leave you. She's just a dumbass Haha I love you booboo
Kynsley	buahaha, love you Nikki ♥ accept my family request!
Andrea	waaaaaaaaah :(whyyy are everyone's friendshipps falling apart?!
Kynsley	because being friends with boys, is better then being friends with fake bitches, but in the end, she'll still be ugly. anywaaaaays♥
Nikki	Okayy
Krissa	i fucking hate you, you stupid whore.
Kynsley	buahahahahahah, some one is clearly upset. your still going to comment on this status ? bahahaha okay :)
Krissa	naaaw dog i just wanted to let you know i fucking hate you you dumb slore. (:
Kynsley	oooh, harsss :) thanks for letting me know "dog". ♥
Krissa	ohh youre welcome dog.& im call you dog cause it looked like you just walked out of the pound. " ♥ "
Kynsley	bahahahha, was that supposed to be mean ? you just sounded dumb, like where did you get that from ? bahaha okay ms. " Krissa " i'm sure you have better things to do, then creep on my status's and defend your "friend", when this all happened last night, your a little late, bye boo boo :)

Krissa	hhahaah your really funnny. But i just wanted to let you know that i hated you like truthfully that is the only reason i commented " ♥ " bye hutch!
Kynsley	that awkward moment when you tell some creepy girl bye and she still replies back trying to get her point through when not a single fuck was given the first time she tried? thanks for expressing your feelings, <333 bye :)
Sandy	I love Jesus.
Kynsley	So do i, i hate everyone else :) just kidding, church together?
Sandy	People need the gracious acts of the lord more than ever. Facebook fights are getting intense.
Kynsley	iNEED, JESUS. :)

Brittney	FAKE ASS MOTHER FUCKING BITCHES...gotta love them. You know who you fucking are you stupid bitch. Happy thanksgiving you dirty ass cunt;)
Tony	ooooooiknow!
Dingdong	Wow
Brittney	-_-
Kendall	Better shut the fuck up bitch. You did the same shit to me.
Brittney	K
Brittney	Difference is im not and never was your friend, so Idont know why your so pissed as if this has ANYTHING to do with you.
Kendall	Cunt, Samantha's my friend. And don't even try talking to kaleb. Hahaha I just think it's sad that you cried to me about you and cole and then you hangout with my ex and expect me to be okay with it. FUNNY.
Eli	fighting on facebook is like the special olympics, because in the end, everyones still retarded :)
Brittney	Hahahahaha she didnt even have to comment it..likesetriously. And im not even mad at the person now

Linsey	apparently David thinks its okay to call girls a "whore" even tho i remember him having a status about respecting girls no matter what. HAHAHAHA hypocrite saywhaaat
David	And don't deny it
David	Therefore your a whore
Stephen	david stop being mean on facebook for real like text her dont be putting stupid stuff that everyone can read on here
David	Did I tag her in a status talking shit? Nah I don't think so
Linsey	stopp being a pussy and answer your phone
Stephen	no but just text her and do drama over texting
Linsey	yes, Stephen is right:)
David	I'm with my mom dude I'll call u later lets meet up bring Brent
David	I'll bring it for your punkass
Stephen	omg David dont fight anyone wtf like seriously you wanna get introuble over this stupid shit?
Linsey	NO. im not fighting David. you're a dumbfuck. BYE
David	It's time for me to earn my respect from these people. I'm over it they pushed me to the limit
Linsey	gtfo
Stephen	okay but seriously you fighting them isn't gunna do anything... no its not ..and kiss the airforce good bye if you get caught
David	I'm a pussy yet you won't say it to me AND leti to our faces. Your a joke
Cassidy	its so manly to fight a girl half your size. its rude to call a girl that and didnt you date her? Sorry you have to prove your manliness like this LOL. love you Linsey ♥
Dave	Haha
David	Someone hit me up I feel like getting down, any of linsey's 5 boyfriends
Linsey	leti is not in this what so ever. you're the asshole here. just shut up and, never talk to me again. if you do, i will litterally call the cops, so for the last time, leave me alone. andi have ONE boyfriend.
Cassidy	sorry to step in again, but five boyfriends? what about the five girlfriends you have?

Linsey	lololololi fucking love you Cassidy ♥ like SOOOO much!
David	You don't know what the situation is I'm tryna fight Brent but he's a pussy and let's his gf fight his battles
David	I have one
David	And i didn't start this but I'm going to finish it when I see Brent
Linsey	thats not true at all David. you started this with me, Brent wasnt in the equation ever. NOW GTFO
Linsey	you're never going to see him, and im sure fighting with a girl is gonna make you seem like such a hardass. Kbye
Cassidy	I love you too baby♥ and I doubt that, hes actually a good guy. and Linsey is just a girlfriend who cares about her boyfriend. and that 'one' girlfriend of yours... you better hope shell do this for you or she doesnt care. and fighting him will do nothing lolwooow its like 6 year olds on the play ground. welldone.
David	Yes I will and never said I was going to fight you but my girl will
Cassidy	then your girl is just as immature as you are. sounds like a perf couple ♥
Linsey	im not fighting anyone. you're harrassing me. and im gonna show "your girl" our texts. so have fun being forever alone. LOLOLOLOL IM DONE HERE. andhahahahh Cassidy i wish i could like your comments 10million timess.
David	I'm going to find Brent, Idgaf
Linsey	have fun with that, in the mean time. get the fuck off my status.
Stephen	omg David seriously don't
Cassidy	what will you want after? a medal for Im such a hard ass? cool. and OMG Linsey Im like in love with you ahahahah saved texts? omg. amazing♥
Linsey	ahahahaahah dude no Cassidy i love you wayyyy more. likeforrreal we need to hangout like right this second coz i hate everyone besides you Brent Stephen and all the people who liked this status♥
Daniel	Yay I liked it
Cassidy	YES! sooon♥i miss youuuu!

David	No more talking. Action time now. Cassidy why are u talking shit I thought we were friends?
Linsey	yayi love you daniel and i miss you too Cassidy! and David, Cassidy is just looking out for me. shes def more my friend than she is yours.
Linsey	and David, no talking and no action. im done with you and ireallydontwanna see your face ever again. BYEEEE for the billionth time
Cassidy	you asked for my number once on fb? I love my Linsey♥ we are still friends but dont be a moron just because you can. dont you think youre maybe better than this? lolidk. youre not proving anything by calling her a whore and fighting her boyfriend will do what? its really stupid you would even bring that up. youre 19. dont you think those should be your high school days? just saying baby♥
David	Well I came into this alone and left alone. I don't need 3 friends to back me on afb fight. I just know you are all bark no bite
Stephen	i think that every one should calm the fuck down like asap! im not backing anyone up i just think this is soooostupid
David	Later :)
Linsey	yessssiiir, i am all bark no bite. i do not fight. now go pretend that you're actually going into the airforce like you always do even tho we all know everytime your day comes to leave it gets "delayed" hahaha bye:)
Cassidy	if you read the convo before this, love, you will see she doesnt need to be 'bite' because she can use her brain and speak words. not throw a punch.
David	I actually have a waivor for a ticket for possession and battery and assault which is why I cnt get cleared for bootcamp but ok
Linsey	ahaha oh yeah, assault was for fucking that one girl in public haha. and oh gooodness i cannot describe how much i adore you Cassidy <33333
David	No I didn't get a ticket for that
Stephen	David Linsey your better than all this come on ... lets hug and make up! like people in this town do
Lauren	OhmyGod, Linsey, I love you♥ Be my best friend hahaha

Linsey	oh..k. hahaha. and Lauren,yes!♥ love you tooo!:
David	Lol
Lauren	I'm a fat ugly whore according to him so don't trip about anything he says. His best friend doesn't even take him seriously. No one does haha
David	Lauren you talked so much shit on Linsey don't even start
Stephen	ohhhh hold up dont talk shit on him. hahha
Lauren	People resolve their problems bro. Grow up like the rest of us have.
Cassidy	is there such thing as learning from mistakes? battery and assault? nobueno, mi vidas. maturity is just needed here. we still love you David but seriously, stop and think what youre doing here. I doubt you actually want her out of your life. just something to think about.
Lauren	Cassidy, I love how mature and helpful you are, but people that don't think there is a problem or don't want to fix their problem, can't be helped.
Cassidy	always hope ♥ just trying to see if maybe somethings can be thought about more. oh well... I love you Linsey. I love you David. ♥♥
Linsey	but i've talked shit on Lauren too. what matters now is that we are friends♥ and Cassidy you're like jesus♥i love you
Cassidy	ahahahahhaomg your so funny♥
Lauren	Oh my God, I've actually said that before. Hahah Cassidy, everyone thinks yourejesus♥
Cassidy	both of you are ridiculous. lol we need a sleepover!
Linsey	yes!!!♥ please. thisweeek!
Cassidy	I leave to hawaii on wednesday!
Lauren	The only thing I have scheduled is sleep for the next week before my life is ended by that nasty thing called school haha so I'm free(:
Cassidy	we will figure it out babies♥
Linsey	k so i think we should monday night! :)
Lauren	Umm if Tasha can come too..haha We have plans(:
Lauren	Haha okay, well thank you for making my day a little brighter knowing I'm not the only one who thinks David is a whore♥haha I love you both. Ttyl.

Linsey	hahahahah love you Lauren ♥ text me sometime girl :)
Lauren	Okay(:
Sean	thats messed up
Linsey	Ahahah thanks Sean:) I agree
Joseph	hahai think its funny how everyone just ganged up on him.. your good friends
Lauren	You're*
Linsey	Hahahahaha I know right Joseph:) ♥
Kynsley	oh Linsey!
Linsey	Oh hi Kynsley ♥
Hazel	bahahaha getting assault for fucking in public? was she younger than the usual fresh man???
David	there's a reason you have the nickname you have.
Linsey	Hahahahah, it was with lynn. And ahah true.
Georgina	David, there's a reason you have the nickname you have.
David	Alright
Hazel	oh shieeet. droppin names haha
David	Hazel who are you?
David	Haha this was between me and Linsey
Hazel	hahah David IM NOT TALKING TO YOU. THAT was between ME and Linsey.
David	Alright.
Linsey	Ahah it really should've been between me and David in the first place coz I probs shouldn't have even written this status... But reallly...who are you Hazel?
David	Agree with Linsey this was mine and hers ordeal
Linsey	Yay, we agree on something haha. K I'm gonna delete this status now before any other randoms comment on it.
Hazel	Im just arizona trailer trash :) according to David
David	Hazel do you feel better about yourself now
Hazel	i do :)
David	Cool well no one really knows who you are... Just sayin
Linsey	i remember her now actually, she was in my pe period. but anyways, thats beside the point. Just sayin its not fun to be called names David.
Hazel	Haha my heart is broken.

David	How do you think I feel to have Like 20 people ganging up on me
Linsey	k, not very goood i guess..i think you should just text me so we can at least be civil with each other.
Hazel	maybe if u were nicer to people David they wouldnt have a reason to gang up on you. justsayin. u say some shitty stuff to people.
Hazel	including myself!
David	K.... And Linsey alright
Hazel	Well the MAN is going to do his normal TRAILER TRASHY shit that i normally do with my TWO friends that i have. Ill message u Linsey
Linsey	Which are total lies btw coz your gorgeous and probs have a million friends coz of how nice you are♥ but okaaay:)
David	Hazel just give up, save your breath if you are going to come at me calling me a pedophile I'm gunna tell you what I think about you, it's only fair
Hazel	hahaha hey u said all that shit first then i called u a pedo. just saying. u have to remember the order shit happens.
David	Alright :)
Hazel	♥
Joseph	i cant believe i wasted my time reading threw this haha i wasted like 3 mins reading this Linsey u should of txt cuz my head spining and David getting ganged up sucks i feel for you
Shella	All of the drama in this Town we could be the new jersey shore ;) justtt sayin, i love both of you, and i already know that if you guys were texting it's already solved. :). I'M BACK IN TOWN Linsey WE NEED TO RAGE.!
Linsey	Yeah, we're civil now:) but hahahayesssssss!♥ this week forsure boo :)

Kynsley	you are a slut, to outspoken to give a fuck ♥
Shella	♥

Kynsley	stopcreepin`. But i'm glad you saw it, it is about you after all <33 soo, uhh. Get Outta Here. you're making yourself look dumb little girl.
Shella	LOVEE making myself look dumb, you know me too well. NOT.
Kynsley	okay, so leave. you're annoying as tits. :)
Shella	shouldn't of wrote an annoying status thennnn♥
Kynsley	Ahahah it's like i say go away, and yet you keep coming back? what is this? a joke? ahah, GOOD BYE Shella. Ahhahahahhaha
Shella	right, cause you control my life♥ sorry queen.HA. funny shitt.
Kynsley	Ahahah, did i ever say icontroll your life? Ahahaha, normally when someone says GO AWAY, the other person should get the feeling that they should leave especially when their annoying af and i'm not tryna deal with little kid bullshit, i called you a slut, GET OVER IT AND GET OUT, ♥:)
Shella	i'm so offended. ....haha
Kynsley	so i stop responding to you on IM, and you go on my comments.... AGAIN. like some people would start to think like some sort of obsession is going on but i'm not really sure what to think, soo give me some time ♥okay? okay :)
Shella	you look like snookie.
Kynsley	and your still IMing me even when istoped replying five minutes ago. awkward, your starting to creep me out, jusaayin.
Kynsley	Shella, CUNTTEEE. get out. can you comprehend that? you're immature.
Marie	why is this chick TRYNA bang on you....you say she looks lyk snookilyk it's a bad thing but then again she's don't look lyk snicks...that thing if fug Kynsley is beautiful! :)
Stacey	Shellaaa, GTFO. i love you kynsley♥
Kynsley	Ahahah thaanks mariee :) iadoreeyouu
Stacey	i love yuu too, eww what thee fuck is this bitches problemm?
Kynsley	hahah, don't knoww :) she's such a hutch, like i really hope Tom wants nothing too do with her, OH BUT HEY, you're mom will hate her even more after this onee :)
Stacey	she already does. along with the rest of us.
Kynsley	i don't know like its one thing to go and write all that shit on your tumblr and make people believe it then break up with your

bf that you supossably lovee sooooo much because you met
*new boys at the football game? And then say you saw the break
up coming and he wasnt worth it? shaddddddddy af, straight up

---

Zoren	**he deleted the post.**

Russell	**i know what a pussy**
Gwyneth	**he ALWAYS does!!**
Zoren	**nigga knows better then to fuck with me**
Russell	**he be scared**
Zoren	**ima still whoop his ass there**
Zoren	**that little shit deleted me**
Russell	**what a bitch**
Zoren	**ima write bitch on his head after i knock his ass out**
Gwyneth	**I love y'all hahah**
Russell	**Cane ur Zoren's bitch**
Zoren	**yeah he is.**
Gwyneth	**Zoren nation >noint nation**
Zoren	**noint nation is my bitch to son.**
Russell	**fuck all those wannab bitches**
Zoren	**yeah son. i fight all of there ass's**
Russell	**they doneee**
Zoren	**ill try any of them**

Brittney	**FRESHMAN BITCH FIGHTS AWWW YYEEAHHHHH**

Helen	**hahahaha freshman are stupid..i swear**
Gayle	**WHAT?!?!?!when was this**
Brittney	**Hahahaha stacey's status**
Stacey	**uh**
McKenzie	**remember those two bitches that fought for pure entertainment? haha we need more people like that in our lives**
Melissa	**I'm literally just sitting here reading it all. Probably the best part of my day.**

Helen	they should make a tv series.. FRESHMAN SHOW DOWWWN hahahaiswear that'd be a hit series
Brittney	Im not making fun hahah stacey id be pissed and do the same thing..soentertaining
Brittney	HAHAHA yes mckenzie!!
Stacey	hahahayeahhi was mad, ahah normally idgaf but he was my boyfriend of over a yearrahah it blowss!
Brittney	Trustt me i know exaactly how that fucking is

Adam	**Hates this wack generation**

Elizabeth	agreed.
Adam	Right..
Hamilton	dont worry il do sumthn awesome with a guitar..,
Adam	Ya like stick up your ass ...
Hamilton	thats ur idea of a show not mine, iv got a lil pride for this wack generation n ima make it beter with some phycadellic guitar
Scott	fucking loser
Hamilton	i agree. its the only thing i can kick ass at tho.i play 20 hrs a day
Adam	And you still suck fag
Hamilton	i dont even know what that means
Lynda	it means you suck at everything in life, like coming up with all the bullshit stories and basically your life in general.
Hamilton	Destiny ive forgotton more than youl ever know..
Lynda	proves your a retard
Scott	haha dont make him slit his wrists for christ sake
Nancy	Amen XD
Scott	dumb bitch ^^ -_-
Nancy	ha you dont even know me dude.
Scott	thank god
Nancy	ohky keep talking shit. thats cool shows how much of a life you have.
Scott	Grow up slut
Nancy	oh yea im the one being immature look whose talking shit dude obviously not me because i dont pick fights with people for no reason exsoecially with people i dont even fucking

	know. and im not a slut. youve prolly slept with more people than i have and i can garanfuckingtee that dude. You need to grow the fuck up but its fine you can still talk shit what else you got to say hiding through a computer screen dude?
Hamilton	You have to forget about what other people say, when you're supposed to die, or when you're supposed to be loving. You have to forget about all these things.
Arthur	u mad?
Nancy	BAHAHAH XD
Bradwin	SO MUCH MAD IT'S HILARIOUS
Hamilton	I'm gonna put a curse on scott and all his kids will be born completely naked.
Ketchie	Hahaha
Clara	Hahaha Jerry Jerry Jerry take yo top off bitcchhessssss JK♥
Adam	Haha crazy
Rylan	WE TRIPPIN MAYNE

Linsey	when me and my best friends clothes won't stay on while jumping on the trampoline. come to my house. I love my life :)

Cherry	Daniel wants to go to your house cuz your clothes are off
Daniel	fuck you guys haha
Aiza	Lololol
David	Fuck facebook
Cherry	Uh?
Daniel	uh......
Linsey	ahaha love you David:)
Rylie	lolwut?:o
Aiza	Def not jumping on the trampoline naked AWK
Linsey	I'm confused. K I hate facefuck. Bye
Rylie	ohsup Linsey.
Linsey	Ahahha exactly Aiza! Everyone stripppin♥aahah hi Rylie:)
David	My notifications are old now. I shoulda never commented on this -_-
Rylie	add me David?^:o

Linsey	Lolwut I thought you guys hated each other...why would he add you?
David	Rylie is a fucking pussy I do hate that kid.
Rylie	uhhhwhat?
Linsey	Awkaf
David	Linsey we agreed to be friends then I go on Britneys status and her and mitch are talkin shit saying I get at young girls and shit haha like okay at least I don't obsess over 8th graders
Rylie	I just laughed, It doesn't mean I agreed with him David, your too quick to jump on me for doing nothing.
Linsey	Rylie...you said "what he said" lol k I'm pretty sure that's agreeing..js.
David	Yeah and he wonders why I wanna beef it with him all the time. It's not my fault the girl you obsess over loves me...
Rylie	damn, drop it already?^ damn. some shit just never drops with you. goodlord.
David	Drop you already*
Rylie	is that going to make you feel good and better about yourself?

Richard	this is what happens when Aaron sees an etch a sketch.

Theresa	... what does it say?
Richard	it says Richard
Theresa	hahaha oh!(:
Dennis	awkward.
Linsey	aww youu are sooocutee♥ :)
Tony	Rylie wouldn't approve...but i do because i completely agree ♥
Linsey	ahaha, yeah Rylie would be like wtf. but i couldnt resist. :)
Rylie	awkward......
Tony	:(
Linsey	Ooh...hmmmm... /: sorry..
Tony	AWK ^^^
Linsey	Verrryyy awk Tony, ahahah
Rylie	Just a bit...
Richard	hi
Linsey	Awk. Hi Richard....

Richard	i'm surprised Rylie saw that haha
Linsey	ahahahahyaa...out of all the pictures on fb. Ahah. That would happen to me.
Richard	oh well i can delete this whole thing and say you got hacked haha
Linsey	Ahahahahahahah....idc. Rylie gets these notifications too tho....lol :P
Richard	true ahaha oh well/:
Linsey	Ahahahnbd. :)
Rylie	:S
Tony	YOU GUYS ARE FUCKIN AWK AND RETARDED!!! ^^^
Linsey	Thanks Tony. We love you too.
Rylie	can you plese text me Linsey ♥?
David	Lol faggits these days
David	And no I don't mean you Richard :)
David	Or Tony or Linsey or aaron... Lmao
Rylie	not like we didn't already know who this was directed at^
David	We all knew faggle
Rylie	cute word
Rylie	how old are you?
David	Shut the fuck up pussy
Tony	hes 19 but why does that matter? ahahaha
Rylie	here comes the crew.^
Tony	here comes the vons crew.^ ready to check me out?:)
Rylie	nah bro, ready to make money, and pursue in life, and not be a low life druggie.
David	Tony this kid thinks he's hard
Rylie	keepin it reall bro.
Tony	so you arent part of the vons crew anymore? andi do have a job and have been sober for 3 days...and im gonna be sober for quite some time because i got caught up in it all
David	Rylie you look like a goofy noodle and work at vons. Get over yourself and maybe get over Linsey too since she went for me and Tony while you were still on her nuts
Rylie	over it bro!
Tony	i asked you how you were doing just trying to be friendly like the last day of school and i guess you knew about me

	and Linsey so you gave me attitude and acted really snobby towards me and walked away and seemed all butthurt....:(you don't exactly seem over it bro..
David	Turn gay already, wait... Too late
David	He talked shit on me all the time which is why I wanna sock this nigga up
Rylie	You act like you never did the same to me^
Tony	awk...
David	I talked shit directly to you, I've no shame
Tony	Richard SHOULD STAY UP!
David	Have no shame fool
Rylie	not directly to me, after we talked. i called Linsey, then i heard you called me a bitch. just after we talked, and said we were cool. thats not directly to my face fool. fuck the rumors. homies>girls drama. we're bigger than this. shits the past. damnn.
David	Richard is a gangsta
David	Homies? Lol, Tonys a homie, someone I can rely on and give personal info to, your a self centered poser who just so happened to be obsessed with my ex girlfriend while we were dating. Nuff said.
Tony	so about Richard...its funny cuz he was with Linsey before all of us xD
David	I know haha he's clearly more experienced
Rylie	waste of typing, dude, over it. it's the past. if your just gunna keep a grudge for nothin, then fine, but it just makes no sense when I got nothin against you.
Rylie	I dont get when you "say shit to my face" comments above, you call me a faggot. I dont understand that either. just a heads up.
David	I don't understand why you think your black.
Linsey	lets all be friends♥ ha i love you BFF. andi miss you David! and Rylie, im glad we are both moved on. (: oh and Richard i still think this picture is sooo fucking cute hahahah
David	Miss you too, and no fuck that haha Rylie is a pussy, i have no respect for pathetic individuals, & Tony text me it's important ♥
Linsey	whats Tony's #?

Tony	555-5555
Richard	HAHAHAHAHAHAHAHAHAHAHAHAHAHAHAHA
Linsey	he meant Rylie
Linsey	...awk
Richard	Oh okay haha
David	Rylie, and Richard I hear you and Darius had a sword fight? ;)
Richard	Hahaha yeah it was pretty hot ;)
Cecilia	David is a puzzi
Fernan	everybody in town is looking at this shit.
Richard	I really hope so
Trey	i love everybody
David	Hahaha let's scrap mothefuckers!!;D
Richard	fsu

Richard	Lol @ when your ex downgrades.
Rowena	whos your ex?
Eli	LOL @ Poodles
Aaron	Justine
Cynthia	-_- you're not funny Eli.
Eli	o
Cynthia	o.... like oxygen
Eli	o
Alexis	i love Justine & she's pretttty :)
Eli	Richard's dad, begs to differ ^
Cynthia	nobody cares
Alexis	thats a little rude Eli, especially over facebook.
Eli	im hardcore though
Cynthia	oh please.
Eli	lol
Eli	say goodnight
Paolo	i like justine. alot.
Peter	Justine is my ♥
Rolly	ahaha how is this about Eli at all? silly people
Carissa	isn't it funny how you went up to justine saying dont post stuff about me on facebook.....awkward how you go and post stuff

	about her. Honestly, this status makes it really obvious that you're jealous of their relationship and Justine is extremely happy, way happier then she ever was with you. So instead of insulting her boyfriend over facebook, why don't you move on with your life. Eli - Your just mad because you cant get a girl like justine.
Eli	O
Carissa	I DONT SEE WHAT OXYGEN HAS TO DO WITH THIS WE ARENT IN CHEMISTRY
Eli	O
Peter	8=====D~~~~~~~~~~O_O
Carissa	justine has moved on to somebody better. i'm sorry Richard that you STILL can't find anybody. and it's funny how you can't even comment back to these. instead, your friend is. good job(: way to be an official ass Richard.
Richard	Or I wasn't on? And what's there to be jealous of? He's just going to get fucked over like I did.
Paolo	they love each other♥
Richard	Carissa; 1. I'm not jealous. I am over her as a girlfriend and a person and I want no association with her. 2. I was actually told today by several people, who I will not name, that he is a downgrade. 3. I haven't found anyone better because I have not really talked to anyone that interests me. 4. Whether or not this is on Facebook, I would have no problem saying this to her, or willies, face.
Carissa	1. obviously you put yourself in association with her by making a status about her knowing she would get mad about it. 2. who cares what anybody else says! 3. you haven't found anybody better because you still start shit with your ex. 4. if it's no problem telling this to them, why didn't you in the first place? 5. that's a fucked up thing to say to the girl you "loved". why would you want somebody that meant so much to you feel the pain you went thru?. that's all i have to say to you Richard. you're pathetic.
Tanner	k Richard's a good guy and thats all i have to say. Everyone calm down.

Paolo	**Tanner dated justine once for a day♥**
Tanner	**HA.**
Landon	**1. Carissa should stfu 2. Carissa should stfu 3. Carissa really needs to stfu**
Tanner	**hahahahaomg**
Aaron	**I love Richard ♥**
Landon	**Tanner make the photo :) Fuck bitches.... Bros before hoes :)**
Carissa	**who are you? you should not be telling me to stfu. i don't even know you.**
Landon	**who are you? cant you read my name stupid ass?**
Tanner	**LOL @ its facebook, everyone should stop fighting..**
Landon	**lolololololololololololo wut.**
Peter	**uhhh Landon. no one has fully gone to the limit of saying something that disrespectful. and i dont think you should jump into this conversation with intentions to start a fight. so regardless if Carissa is my girlfriend and justine is my bestfriend, you have no right to be this rude without knowing the circumstances or being involved in the argument. so just pick your words wisely bud:)**
Carissa	**it means how do i know you "stupid ass"**
Paolo	**this Landon guy is mean..if he knew Carissa he would fall in love with her like i did♥**
Landon	**why would i try to start a fight with a girl? are you kidding me right now?**
Peter	**not physically. verbally.**
Carissa	**you basically just put yourself in that position. if you tell me to "stfu", do you really think i would ignore that?**
Landon	**maybe if you were mature ^**
Paolo	**shes the most mature freshmen ive ever met.**
Carissa	**dude. you commented on this status when you had no part in it. Gtfo**
Landon	**dude dudedudedudedudedude..... Richard is one of my good friends i have everyright too... so dude you GTFO**
Carissa	**this is justine. ALL OF YOU ON Richard'S SIDE ARE BEING SO RUDE RIGHT NOW. Didn't your mothers teach you any manners? If you have nothing nice to say, don't say anything at all. And to Richard - if you aren't jealous, why in the world**

	would you post this status. Like are you kidding me? A facebook fight? I hope you realize that everyone is on my side on this one. Stop being a snob, and move on.
David	Who wants to fight
Richard	My mother told me you were a heartless bitch hahahahahaha
Paolo	Rylie does aha
Carissa	That was very rude of your mom, and your dad for saying I'm ugly. Good to know that your parents are being immature about this too.
Carissa	now i know where you get it from.
Peter	HAHAHAHAHAHAHAHA Paolo YOU MAKE MY LIFE!
Richard	They're not immature..they just don't like you
David	Richard is a good guy. He's my friend. Fuck bitches get money stay strong my brotha don't let no hoe bring you down
Carissa	David YOU HAVE NEVER EVEN MET ME. anyways, since your parents talked behind my back that shows some immaturity.
Paolo	Peter, you and Carissa make my life hahahaha
Paolo	Carissa David is a good guy, be nice
Richard	And to any of you who think this is for any reason other than humor: you're fucking stupid.
Carissa	this is not funny. this is disrespectful and rude.
Richard	And Carissa, people hate on David a lot but I think he's a good guy. I don't even know him and he's sticking up for me. Don't talk shit to him.
Carissa	THIS IS JUSTINE. THIS ISNT Carissa.
Tanner	LOL^
Carissa	and how is saying "you have never even met me" talking shit? really?
Tanner	LOL^
Aaron	LOL at people who get butt hurt easily
Carissa	Aaron its not getting butt hurt, its downright being bullied. Its not acceptable.
David	Carissa's are bomb.
Richard	You are not being physically harmed in any way, nor do I have an unfair advantage. This is not bullying
Carissa	it's called cyber bullying.

Tanner	**omg just stop....**
Bernadette	**I personally think you should just delete the status. ^^^^^ Facebook drama is just unnecessary.**
Richard	**Hell no! I'm keeping this shit :D**
David	**Bullying would be Richard writing unnecessary shit on your wall no one asked you to comment on this legendary status that will not be deleted LoL**
Carissa	**LoL who are you?**
Rolly	**facebook just brings out the best in everyone! what a wonderful website!**
Tanner	**He's David**
Tori	**omg David......" Carissas are bomb" yesssss that comment made my life**
David	**Haha this Carissa needs a few Carissas to loosen up a bit. So angry I swear!! And who am I?<------- read the name**
Tori	**who doesn't know David..........like honestly tho.**
Richard	**David served my food whaddup bitches**
David	**I'm infamous around town. Haters dont like me but they don't wanna fight me. Hoes wanna judge me when they really wanna fuck me. Call me a douche all you want but I speak the truth on that**
Aaron	**Carissa disappeared :0**
Germa	**justine is amazing an willie is a good guy for her and no offense but its really weird that you keep commenting on her stuff and writing about her on facebook especially when its to make fun of her it just makes you look desperate and its not cool she didnt do anything**
David	**She's printing these to show to the school officer probly so you may be called up tomorrow because your "CYBER BULLYING"**
Richard	**Hahahaha oh my god**
Tanner	**hahahahahaha this happpened at the beginning of the year...**
David	**It's happened to me a lot. I almost got arrested for threatening these kids once. So gay I swear**
Aaron	**Good thing Officer John isn't at our school anymore :)**
Tanner	❖ Σ ⊗ ♒ ♠ Ω ♤ ♣ ♡ ♦ ◇ ♕ ♛ ♖ ♔ ★ ☆ ✦ ★ ⚡ ☾ ☽ ☼ ☀ ☘ ⛱ ☂ ☁ ◉ ⏣ ♪ ✂ ✄

David	Sweet that guy was a monkey spanked I swear.
David	Spanker
Travis	Holy fuck... this status is exactly like Hiroshima... or Nagasaki something
Aaron	Shits dead now hahah
Charlene	ew. Richard get over yourself.
Trent	Tanner
Rolly	just throwin this out there, mrlarry is quite the handsome fellow, not to mention his muscles...
Arvin	LOUD NOISES
Carissa	wow. we are not printing this out so stop. this is a waste of time
Brittney	i can't read any of Davids comments because he blocked me.... my life sucks...and Richard SHE'S A NICE LADY STAHP DAT (stop that)
Rolly	i printed it out though :o
Richard	She's not nice to me...and this is over bye everyone
Brittney	bye bye...♥
Rolly	party over here!
Landon	Hi Brittney
Brittney	bye
Rylie	Paolowait...what?
Rylie	I can't read David's comments, he blocked me LOL.
Landon	bye
Landon	David its kinda funny when you say she's gonna report to officer john.... HIS ASS GOT FIRED A LONG TIME AGO HAHA
Ronan	Carissa, please take one moment to hear me out. Everything you know in high school will completely change once you hit college, that is if you're smart enough to get into one. If not, chances are you will get knocked up by some dirtbag and spend the rest of your life as a lower middle class hoebag. The point is, in high school, love does not exist. It isn't even a real tangible thing yet. 90% of the people you know will forget about you, including the ones you thought you were serious with. Aside from that, my friend Richard here is a really cool dude, and any chick that dumped/broke up with/got dumped by Richard is total and complete whorish cum-dumpster not deserving of life

itself. Anyone that would claim to be friends with such a person including you and her boyfriend can kindly fuck off because you aren't even close to being on a level where you'd be allowed to talk to him. Thanks for your cooperation.

Rylie	school cops can only be school cops for 2 years
Richard	ronan knows whassup!
Landon	Richard's side-34982348970243893256942896 5468 Carissa's side- 0.5
Richard	not to mention every single thing about me that she has said has been inaccurate haha
Landon	W
Landon	I
Landon	N
Landon	N
Landon	I
Landon	N
Landon	G
Bobby	Facebook Fights
Bobby	Can clarissa please come back im tryin to roll bawwlzzzzzz
Rolly	are we fighting again?
Rolly	do i have to re-print this?
Peter	ronan, who the fuck are you to talk to someone that much fucking younger with that much fucking disrespect, especially to a girl. You just talked shit on so many people you dont even fucking know. yes Richard and justine broke up, but why the fuck is that relevant now. it is the past and it shouldnt be brought up because it is no longer important and both of them have moved on. for you to join a conversation and abruptly and rudely state your ignorant and selfless opinion is pretty low. I dont know what satisfaction this has given you, but since you are such a 'matured' college student, how bout you grow the fuck up and get the fuck out of high school drama. because it seems to me there is an absence of maturity in you and you should learn some respect before targeting a freshman high school girl. so watch how you fucking talk cuz eventually it will bite you in the ass when you say it to the wrong person. thanks.

Landon	if you have to say all that... than why are you still here?
Daryl	Well this successfully distracted me from all of my homework.
Peter	Landon, because it disrespected my girlfriend for one, and another reason is you along with many people have been constantly egging this argument on and blowing up my newsfeed so this shit needs to end. do u guys have nothing better to do. im pretty sure Richard along with the 'opposing side' would love for this to end because once you realize what maturity is you will know that this shit is pointless. and i said that because i have come to realize that a majority of you guys dont know or have been never been taught the word RESPECT. thats why.
Richard	ronan's disrespect toward Carissa was merely a by-product of when he stood up for me.
Richard	I know what respect is, and Justine never gave me any.
Landon	we have a different opinion and say in this Peter.
Peter	I'm not in this to talk about you and her. standing up for you is different than verbally attacking someone dude. i mean i understand how you feel but there is no reason for him to be an asshole to other people he could have just bluntly said his opnion of you instead of insulting others
Landon	i love you.

Lino	Fat niggas are annoying as fuck. I think we all know who I'm talking about.

Brittney	oh myyy..
Gino	yea it really isnt worth it .coolittt
Piyush	#TeamBackfades L
Perseus	Lino your the man
Lino	Nigga you sale fun size bags of chips at school and I'm ratchet? Hahahanigga you got it all fucked up.
Anthony	hahha im getting my fucking money, and your getting what? a bad rep, no one likes you nor your fucking music. go get a fucking life

Lino	Your getting you money???Hahahah you ask people for quarters and shit. And you're getting your money? Hahaha
Perseus	if you aint got haters you aint doin it right
Lino	HAHAHAHAHAH this niggas ridiculous.
Anthony	hahahyepp :D cus i got it like that whats brackin
Lino	Hahaaha you a funny ass nigga man.
Lino	Weird ass nigga
Anthony	hahahahaahahaha, hadnin
Lino	Hahahahanigga said he was getting his money. Hahahaha I'm dying
Anthony	HAHAHAH rap about it nigga. rap A BOUT IT
Julynie	Wow thats rude to just put me on blast like that... ;) haha playin
Lino	I'm talking about this butter ball ass nigga up here ^^^
Anthony	hahaha awe Lino your soo fucking flattering, get a fucking life bitch
Lino	Get a life? Hahahahnigga where's yours?!!
Aileen	"no one likes you nor your fucking music" <------------------- WHAT?!?!?!?!?!?!?!?!?!?!??!?!?!?!?!?!?!?!!are you deaf cuz last time i checked Lino's music is better than sex...........................
Anthony	i got mine no need to worry, awe soo you like sex? Swag
Aileen	ew..
Anthony	ratchetttttttt
Lino	Idk if you do bra. What's your plan after school? Sell chips?
Julynie	Omg... i hate hatred :(well yall have fun with this lil tiff. i know yall are gunna make up sooner or later right???
Anthony	hahah yeah i was actually gonna open up a liquor store.
Piolo	GUCCI!!!
Lino	Hahahahhhahahaahahaahahah
Anthony	put my name in one of your mixtapes im sure you will get money to put into your name!
Piolo	THE JOLLY GREEN GIANT IS GETTING ANGRY >:O
Tony	FUCK THAT FAGGOT^ laughing at me for getting my fuckin car jacked fuck you go suck a dick you faggot ass drama causing bitch
Lino	Kids a douche for that bro. That's only reason he pissed me off. Kinda crossed the line on that. Hope you find your shit Lil bra

Fernan	i really wanna know if Tony's mad at Lino or Anthony..
Piyush	Lino's musiic goes ?
Tony	thanks homie^ just straight disrespect.this is serious shit not some sucking some fools dick behind the store type of shit Anthony
Fernan	oh..that's fucked up Anthony..
Rowell	I bump Lino, and i got 2, 12's in the jeep, bumpin like a mothhhaafuckkaaaa
Gino	i want as many people thats on Lino's dick on mine! notfair haha
Tony	the time just drags when you're waiting for Anthony's next gay ass response
Lino	Gino there's a difference between being on my dick and supporting.
Gino	oh okay , thank u , i was confused .
Lino	Anthony get off my status nigga.
Lino	Go exercise.
Lindy	Lino you dumb afsooo is you Tony taa get off Anthony's head though
Lino	Lindy I have to much respect for you to even come at you. But you need to get off my status
Lindy	Lino I'm just lettttin' you knoow thas the homeboy & lowball you was tooo but talkin all that head on Anthony aint' cooool
Lino	Him being your homeboy has nothing to with this. This between me and bruh. And that nigga is the queen of talking head. Real shit.
Lindy	If it's on FB, it's everyoooones business. Realtalk
Lino	Fasho, if that's how you feel my nigga. But that nigga comes sideways at me so I'm not boutta respect bra no way. If that makes me dumb then you must be dumb too. Cause I know you got some people you don't respect. And that's a fact. B
Lino	But this ain't about you
Lindy	Rufffrufff. lol

Lulu	the fights on my status, are like paragraphs hahahah i love you all.

Lulu	so apparently me & Margie are trashy sluts & people like to post shit on tumblr about us ♥
David	All I got from that was that people have no lives babe
Lauren	your haters make you famous♥ remember that.
Lulu	hahahahah theres hundreds of note & posts about saying how im soo easy, from people i dont even fucking know!!
Margie	Were just too popular I swear(; I don't even know half of them but apprently there in our classes..I feel like I'm gettin stalked ahhahaha
David	Classy haha. Fuckin losers I swear
Lulu	mee too there like oh yeah that chick Lulu was in my pe class last year ... like the fuck alright then.
Lauren	Jealousss obviously. Pretty girls get hot boys and have fun... What does she do? She post crap about your life on Tumblr because she's a loser and doesn't have one♥
Lulu	Awee your so sweet (: &i know ♥ who copy & pastes that shit onto tumblr and then just talks shit just because they can ?! get lives
David	I don't like fat people either their assholes and complain about everything hahaha so I'm on your side fuck those losers
Lexi	...... Lulu i love you but this is probably the most shallow thing i have ever seen.
Lulu	heyy i didnt post it i just said omygawd i love youuu & now everyone is talking shit on me...
Lexi	nonono i wasn't talking about you, I'm just saying there's really no defending this....
Margie	hahaha uhm i can say whatever i want, my opinion didnt ask for yours [:
Lexi	Your opinion is ignorant, shallow, and not worth the time or arguing.
Margie	once again i didnt ask for yourss , you dummbb err whaa?
Lexi	You can state your opinion and I can state mine, guess we'll just have to agree to disagree.
Sherman	Lol I guess tumblr is where it's at now uh day haha
Brittney	ew
Tori	Lexi wins bye

Stacey	Margie i dont even have to know you to say your a shallow twat, and David im going to stick with my opinion that youre a piece of shit. just saying, id rather be OBSESE AND happy and a fucking good person that a skinny shallow twat. love you Lexi
Margie	hahahha ^ its rlly not about winning. i had an opinion that i rlly dont like fat ppl, there fat because they chose to live that way and if you choose to live that way its unhealthy and youll die earlier on in life anywayss. so im sorry you ppl take shit up the ass and take the time to take snap shots and post them on tumblr and talk shit ahhaa
Margie	^^^^^^^^^^^
Tori	Lexi and Stacey's opinon> Margie. Margie is the name of a rabbit on a tv show LOL
Brittney	your a bitch Margie
Lulu	doode i like all of you guys :(just agree to disagree.
Margie	hahaa then i am a bitch, and thats finee with mee sweety[:
Brittney	Okay well you're shallow as fuck that's seriously so fucked up who the hell raised you to be so mean? Ha
Tori	your opinion is irrelevant and you are irrelevant Margie
Stacey	and dont think that your "popular" because people are talking shit on you.
Brittney	hellappopularz
Margie	Brittney: a bigger bitchh. haha Stacey: its a joke . dont get too asshole hurt nowww haha Tori: your irrelevant as well [:
Stacey	How is that even a joke are you stupid?
Tori	nobody asked you to reply
Stacey	you are a joke.
Imelda	Is this a fucking joke or is this girl really that much of a shallow cunt? Haha Lulu you know I love you but your friend is a bitch
Tori	gawt da town bitchez comin' at ya Margie. lawl
Margie	haha okaayyy !andd none of you are no better than me..i dont talk shit on fat ppl i just would rather talk to a skinny person anyday. andd your talking shit on me and i havent rlly said shit to any of you, so have fun talking shit cause you ppl have obviously nothing better to doo

Brittney	YOU JUST FUCKING DID OH MY GOD you are so dumb
David	Stacey hahahaha
Lulu	i lovee you alll & i dont hate fat people.... k byee
Brittney	Nobody's mad at you Lulu ♥ hahaha
David	I used to be fat. y'all are gonna have issues in life if someone elses opinion effects you this much. Losers!!!!
Valerie	Bitches needa stfu. Let's make this simple ;p Keep your negative thoughts to yourself ;p if you don't like them gtf over it .. Move on obviously your jealous or some shit becuz if u weren't u wouldn't be startn shit and who ever is post shit on tumblr is a fucken weird ass stocker tf girls are fucken weird these days.
Brittney	t's not like it hurts my feelings thats just fucked up and that opinion shouldn't be stated publicly because its rude as fuck.. ha
Stacey	David if you used to be fat that you know how bad itd hurt if someone said some shit like this about you. my 7 year old little brother is already being effected by this horrible ass society. when he gets dressed for school and asks me if he looks fat, it breaks my fucking heart. so ill stand by my fucking opinion previously stated
Imelda	This has nothing to do with you talking shit on us but its classless bitches like you that cause girls to receipt eating disorders, depression, and suicidal thoughts. Who the fuck are you to judge someone based on their size.
Stacey	OR BASED ON ANYTHING
David	Stacey thinks it's fucked up to state an opinion of not liking fat people which was a joke, yet she tells me I'm a piece of shit. Hypocrite ? Haha
Imelda	you cant say something like that and call it a joke shes ignorant af
Stacey	WELL FAT PEOPLE COULD BE GOOD PEOPLE AND YOURE NOT A FUCKING GOOD PERSON AND I ACTUALLY KNOW THAT SO.
Valerie	Omg ya it's rude Margie ;p Be nice, BUT GIRLS GET OVER IT SHE MIGHT BE A BIT COLD HEARTED ♥ ;) haha BUT SHE AIN'T TALKIN SPECIFICALLY TO YOU GUYS SO

	WHY COMMENT??? Grow the fuck up, learn to keep ur mouths shut. And do what your mama taught you "just ignore them" c'mon now we learned this in kindergarten t-.-
David	I was fat af ask everyone. Then I decided to use my middle school bullies as motivation and got into boxing. Your brother will make it out of this phase a stronger person trust me
Margie	Yes you know so much about me ..hahahahahaha
Lexi	Well my mother actually taught me not to judge people based on appearance, and to stand up for what is right. That is beyond an opinion that is the kind of hate that drives people to kill themselves. Teen suicide rate is going up, wonder why....
Imelda	if by "stronger person" you mean he'll turn out like you then thats not a good thing David. nobody should have to be put through anything like that
David	Teen Suicide is going up I agree. People always try and bring me down and y'all know that's a fact. So instead of going back and forth with insults just move on and AGREE TO DISAGREE. This is a big world and this cyber bullshit is fucking annoying. Jussayin and honestly everyone on this status excluding Lexi, my girlfriend, Margie and the others from that other city have said nasty fucked up shit about me. Especially Imelda, Stacey and Brittney
Valerie	SHHUUUTTT UP!!!!! I NEEVER ONCE SAID IT WAS OK OR ANYTHING LIKE THAT I DON'T EVEN AGREE WITH WHAT THEY ARE SAYING BUT SERIOUSLY YOU GUYS NEED TO JUSTT STOP WITH ALL THIS. GETTIN ALL WORKED UP OVER STUPID COMMENTS IS SO POINTLESS. NO JOKE THIS IS A POINTLESS FUXKEN ARGUMENT. -.-
Valerie	BE "STRONG" people and learned to not let stupid shit get to u!!
David	Imelda you don't know me or what I have been through your a little spoiled bitch on the real. I may be known as a player and tool in this town but maybe because it's filled with girls like you who expect to be treated like women…When they just act like spoiled stuck up bitches.

Valerie	And ya I agree this Imelda bitches comment are kinda annoying.
David	Fuck the haters y'all
David	I would rather be real and an asshole then a fake bitch like all of our towns female population
Lexi	Okay, this is not going anywhere. I just don't understand some people. And yes bullying happens all the time, but back in the 1940's so did the holocaust because Hitler hated jews. Simple innocent people discriminated against, made victims of mass murder. why? because Hitler was a hateful son of a bitch. Just because something can't be stopped doesn't mean you should join the cause. It means you should stand up against it so that someone knows there are people out there who won't judge them and consider them equal.
Margie	Yeah imma go shoot all fat people.
Lexi	No, you'll just say you hate them and make them feel worthless because you can
Valerie	Yeah imma go shoot all the bitches who can't shut up instead ;p
Margie	Are you fat or something? Hahahaha
Imelda	Fuck off David. You don't know shit about me or anything going on in my life. I don't give a fuck if I come off as a bitch. David I genuinely apologized to you for talking shit... but alrighty. I was directing my comments more towards Margie haa
Margie	Okay she can come off as a bitch but I can't ^ ALRIGHT THEN.
Brittney	think....that if you had worded what you said in a nicer way, no one would be mad ha that's just my opinion tho
Tori	she's being a bitch for the right reasons and you're being a bitch for the wrong reasons. el stupiddoooooo
Lexi	Ya know what, I am. But I would rather be fat or chubby than on the same level as a nazi. I hope one day you'll be able to see that hate is not something to be proud of. But I'm not worried you'll get exactly what's coming to you because life is karma. Hitler sure did. (; and yeah I did compare you to Hitler because he was a hateful, bitter, monster just like YOU.

Brittney	MONSTER Tori
Sherman	Damn I've never read so much in my life this should be a book haha my momma would be proud :P
Tori	Lexi you are NOT fat. and even if you were you'd still be beautiful in my book. and you have an amazing personality that beats skinnyness ANYDAY. and everyone would fucking agree with that...♥
Tori	MONSTER! i wanna tag curtis lol but i'm not going too...
Brittney	I AGREE I AGREE!
Brittney	Haaa he's making bad decisions at the moment lawlz :/
Tori	oh gawd curtis.......
Margie	Hmmm. Never had karma, Im just a lucky girl. Bein on the same level as a Nazi would be mean id have to kill what I hate. Where do you live? I have to kill u now, because your fat & all ya know
Stacey	i am a bitch, straight up. especially when it comes to ignorance. i cant stand that shit. no person is better or worse based off of physical traits. love you Lexi, you are gorgeous. inside and out
Tori	thats a threat rabbit girl... someone call da cops er sumthen
Brittney	Why do you continue to say mean shit uh
Lexi	Ohh death threat, keep going your making yourself look better and better.
David	Imelda idgaf what you or anyone else thinks. In MY OPINION. Your a bitch and it's okay for you to be one but not anyone else? Haha k
Tori	NOBODY LIKES YOU ON THIS STATUS. YOU DON'T LOOK COOL AT ALL. GOD FUCKING DAMN BITCH GIVE THE FUCK UP
Tori	except David and Lulu LAWL
Margie	Hahaha yes I threatened your ass (; Me ? Say mean shit? Haha okay after ppl have said mean shit to me and you all expect me just walk away? Doesn't work like that sorry
Brittney	You're just making yourself look worse haaaa
Stacey	the earth would be better if people like you didnt walk it.
Tori	you wonder why people write mean shit about you on tumblr ha

Lexi	I hope you know if I called the cops right now you would be put in jail... ha your not very intelligent. So for your sake I would shut the hell up.
Margie	I rlly couldn't care how I look to you people hahaha
Tori	obviously you do since ya keep replying babbygirl
Melissa	Um hi everyone. i don't want to get in this drama cus i love you all but I dont know if you know this Margie but a lot of people will develop eating disorders and depression and a lot of other things from that comment alone. people come in many different shapes and sizes and they are all beautiful. the size of your pants and the number on the scale does not define someone. you need to be careful what you say because some people will actually take that to heart. and one of my best friends is over weight and she is one of the sweetest people i know. you cant judge someone by their weight. some people can't control it. not everyone is meant to be a size 00. and Lexi you dont even fall into the fat category and you're gorgeous as fuck bb ♥ okay bye nowwwww!
Valerie	Okay this Tori bitch is a joke ;D hahahaha !!! Hahahah dumb bitch you got girls from all over after you now. Ahahaha I've got family and friends every where don't be stupid now I can't believe you'd even say that hahaha wanna be cholita over here.
Margie	Lexi you would be arrested as well
Lexi	This is the girl you people are defending? This girl who is literally threatening to kill me because I'm spreading the love?? SMART.
Stacey	even if you were the most gorgeous girl in the world, youre actions make you apear to be the UGLIEST
Tori	yee gurl imma cholita im finna kick ur ass bb. lawl jk not about to deny that i'm a little white girl who is faaar from a chola so i dont know what the fuck you're talking about Valerie
Margie	Your not spreading the love...you ppl started talking shit on me first so that's obviously starting something instead of ending or resolving it
Brittney	Because you're fucked up ha
David	I respect all of you except Imelda and I just lost respect for Stacey. If I was such a piece of shit would I have beat wades ass

	for you and all your friends and send him to rehab?? Think about it I didn't do that for myself. But yup I'm such a bad person. Whatever
Lexi	Girl, you should stay in your city because no one here wants your judgement or ignorance anywhere around them. Oh and you need some help because threatening to kill someone isn't considered sane on any level. You obviously have some confidence issues that you need to work out and stop taking your anger out on others. You have the problem NOT them
Valerie	Then bitch get some thicker eye brows and don't fucken bring up cities and shit. Now your one ignorant fool you bitches wanna talk about being ignorant shit. You guys are if you were smarter you would have just kept ur mouth shut.
Brittney	Remember the good ol' days when people used to get jumped for their milk money & not cuz of Facebook fights?...lawlz I do...
Margie	My confidence is through the roof. You just keep talking shit but you can't answer simple questions so you continue to work around them. Your no better than me(: I'm done here. Later (;
Brittney	c u next Thursday
Rodrigo	WAIT WHO IS ARGUING WITH WHO?! i am lost…
Lexi	Well then, you try and walk around with your head up high making comments like that, because I'm pretty sure if you say it to the wrong "fat" person they might kick your skinny ass.
Tori	lawl im really fucking confused tho
Valerie	everyone is just venting ;p
Rodrigo	Ohhhhhhhhh, okay keep doing it..it's entertaining me :)
Valerie	Haha k love u nd my mom say hi ;pp
David	No one jumps me for facebook shit cuz ttown is a bunch of pussys. My bros seem to be the only real niggas in this town. My homegirl and even Linsey is down. They seem to be the only girls who throw down here. So I wouldnt go acting hard and start trippin on ctown cuz that's ignorant af. Aight I'm done too
Tori	who is trippin on ctown I AM SO FUCKING CONFUSED
Stacey	oh yeah David beating wades ass REALLY FUCKING MADE MY LIFE BETTER. i dont believe in violence. if anything your a shitty friend for just flipping the scripton wade like that. not that i like wade at all it just says alot about your character. i

dont need the respect of someone who doesnt have enough respect for himself to keep his dick in his pants. im done here we all know who the 'real" people are and who they arent.. love most of you bye ♥

Brittney wade stole my purse......HEY STACEY ILY

Lexi David I like you, but to be honest it's kind of disapointing to see you say all this stuff after all the hell you've been put through. Please just think about how you felt, and if you would really want to be responsible for making others feel like that. Maybe you can handle it but not everyone can. Just think about it....I'm done. Goodnight

David Stacey, Wade deserved what he got. Little punk ass bitch called me out in front of my grandma and I knocked him the fuck out so you can't make me feel bad about that shit. From what I hear you can't keep your panties on either and your quite provocative so like I said we can just agree to disagree and dislike each other. I'm out

David Lexi I used to be fat. I don't ever bully people by their appearance I swear. I just think that some overweight people feel sorry for themselves instead of do something about it. I don't tell them to kill themselves cuz they are fat or ugly.

Stacey funnyy because i dont even hook up with people lol. and the only people ive had sex with ive loved WHICH IS HOW IT SHOULD BE. youre a shitty toxic person David,

Stacey goodbye

Lexi Easier said than done, a lot of them struggle with mental disorders. And for some it's an eating disorder just like anorexia. And for others it's the only comfort they have because the world is just too much. Okay I'm really done now.

Lulu I know your a good guy at heart, please show everyone else that. Night guys love everone, that i know, and has a brain. ♥

David Hahaha I'm a shitty toxic person? Because I've done you so wrong right? I barely even know you. You just hate on me all the time but it doesn't phase me. Haters make me stronger and I'm proud to say I handle my shit on my own. Nobody fights my battles for me. And fasho late

Stacey loz i said bye can you read

David	**Night Lexi ♥**
Archie	**i really wanna read all this but im trynna sleep in 10 mins**
David	**I can read just thought I would let you know your comment was irrelevant and obviously an opinion that was meant to be hurtful when really I just Lold cuz you dont know me. K bye(:**
Debbie	**This is comedy love Lulu and Margie ♥**
Geraldine	**Haha Archie I was about to say that. I don't want to drag my ass into any bullshit, but this is all immature. Sure what Margie said was fucked up but she's entitled to her own opinion, as well as the rest of us, but going and talking about it will just make shit worse. Be the bigger person and stop butting heads over something so stupid. Not that anyone asked but thats just my 2cents.**

Drake	**All guys aren't liars, every girl is just gullible.**
Imelda	**not every girl :)**
Drake	**That kind of comment is most expected after the creation of a post like this haha**
Bryce	**not errrry girl, dooode.**
Gloria	**Wouldn't the guy have to lie for a girl to be gullible? O.o**
Drake	**Girls will believe anything they hear whether it's a lie or not**
Princess	**guys believe everything too, trust me :)**
Bryce	**so if theres nothing wrong with believeing truth, you have to be gullible to believe the lies, which means. the guys lieiiinnn'**
Yasmin	**Its ridiculous how many likes yu got because this post does not even make sense. Being gullible is believing things that are not true. Every girl is not gullible, you stupid, please delete me because your posts annoy the fuck out of me. Thanks.**
Drake	**Which makes it equally the girls fault for being gullible enough to believe it ;)**
Drake	**Hahahaha Yasmin don't cry now**
Yasmin	**every girl is gullible, not all guys are liars, your stupid, and so is everyone that liked this. It's a contradiction.**
Drake	**Are you going to cry?**
Yasmin	**Are yu fucking stupid?**

Yasmin	Girls, let's just like this and call our sex gullible. Fuckin stupid haha delete me! I don't even know yu I dont know how yu got on my friends list and your posts annoy me.
Joyce	Are you gullible?^
Yasmin	Why would you ask that?^
Drake	She must be... She hates me but she wants me to delete her... Hahah
Arceli	when a girl believes a guy's lie, it doesn't mean she's gullible. it means she thought she could trust someone who meant a lot to her.
Drake	okay doctor phil
Arceli	i should start my own show
Drake	Call it doctor pastors daughter
Arceli	stfu
Yasmin	Because my phone will not let me, god yur annoying ignorant little boy delete me.
Drake	hahaha lah you brontizzle
Drake	Dont get your little chonies in a twist, we can settle our differences peacefully.
Gloria	My comment is the best. Everyone just stop commenting. I win. ♥ Hahahaha just kidding :) But seriously guys, shut up. I hate fighting, especially over facebook haha
Yasmin	Just delete me, I honestly don't want to see yur immature, absent minded posts any longer.
Drake	Can we cry a little bit more?
Arceli	why can't we be friends
Yasmin	Look, yur ugly, yur annoying, yur fucking young, just delete me
Drake	Aw now your going to make me cry :(
Yasmin	Waaaaaaaahhhhhhhhh. FUCKING DELETE ME YOUR FUCKING ANNOYING.
Drake	And you still keep talking haha...
Yasmin	^little girl, I'd keep yur mouth shut ;)
Drake	Yasmin your supposed to be crying not talking
Gina	lawl yer tramatizn him staph et rahn

Gloria	You can delete him off your phone. Just click the 3 lines on the top left. Scroll down to desktop site. Go to his profile and delete him. Now can we please stop talking?
Yasmin	Shut the fuck up, I'd love to see youuuuuu little boy.
Drake	I think someone ran out of midol this morning...
Yasmin	Yu too little girl (;
Yasmin	Yeah I think so too, that must be why your posts are extra fucking annoying today (:
Drake	I now know why your so pissy, you ran out of midol and this post actually happens to relate to you as of 6 hours ago...
Yasmin	I'm nineteen and have no idea why the fuck this kid is on my friends or how he got there. I will speak my mind, and ask yu once again to delete me, if I could I sure as hell would.
Arceli	uhhh, Drake is 18. you're one year older. big woop. your mom didn't seem to think he was too young....
Yasmin	Arceli, watever name that is, were not friends so yu don't see my posts dumbass.
Yasmin	Ohhhhhhh good one Arceli, but my mom died a few months ago. ;)
Yasmin	Oh please, let's all get butthurt because I ask this annoying fuck to delete me (;
Yasmin	obviously if my phone let me delete him I would. Now shut the fuck up because I wasn't talking to you.
Drake	I like turtles
Benedict	all you lil niggas are trippin over some facebook bullshit, go fuck yourselves.
Drake	MY NIGGA
Gloria	Please follow my instructions as written. Thank you and goodnight.
Drake	She did it, I'm so proud
Gloria	♥
Sarane	you speak the truth
Girlie	This whole thing is hilarious ♥
Nova	Ummmm , i don't know any of you . but Drake's posts make me laugh , if you wanna get all butthurt over it , then do it in your own little world....you just wasted your time , because no

	one cares . if you get this mad over a Facebook post....you've got some issues....
Girlie	^couldn't agree more.
Walter	Deffff got I like turtles stuck in your head today ;)
Tope	so how bout that facebook porn Drake...
Drake	I wish those pictures were you :(

Drake	When someone deletes you because they made themselves look stupid... okay hahahah
Brittney	Lauren?.....
Drake	ewaaahhh
Brittney	what
Drake	Her. She gross
Brittney	Hahahahhahahahahah omg
Drake	Did you see that earlier? We were talking about relationships and some how it was like rape?
Brittney	Hhahahahahh yes
Drake	than she got pissed cause her arguments were invalid, deleted me and all our comments proving her stupidity.
Brittney	HAHAHAHAHHAHAHA so typical tho
Drake	Hahaha I knowwwwwwww fb bichez these days

Franklin	love how my ex girlfriend cares so much about what i do. haha im so glad i like a new girl :)
Janee	haha Franklin you're such a douche sometimes.
Mariphel	Shutttttupppppp. How immature can you get? #thingsthatdontneedtobeonfacebook
Franklin	Hahahahah
Rico	#peoplewhoputpoundsignsinfrontofasentence withoutspacesareannoying
Rylie	LOL.
Dante	iwouldnt personally put this on facebookcuz it should be between u two haha but happy for you fool

Myra	Happy for you Franklin(:
Mariphel	Jeeeeeeze RicoI dont even know, #rude hahahahahahhahaha
Franklin	haha love u Rico :)
Mariphel	Dont even know you*
Mariphel	Lawlz.
Janelle	Sofuckin chill dude. Probably gonna cheat on this "new girl" too. #sorry bout it
Hazel	wow haha I love this ♥
Hazel	Even the ones who u didnt date are jumping down ur throat :) Someones got game bahaha
Franklin	Thanks! Mariphel moved on too! She has rick! hope the best to them :)
Hazel	iwouldnt want my nick name to be bang....lol
Franklin	Hahahaha
Hazel	Disgusted>jelaous. Hahahahaha
JV	Ur a fuckenidiot.. Bang posted everything on Facebook. Like finally she stopped crying about it..
Myra	HahahaomgLolz so happy for you Franklin, jealousy is a bitch♥ Btw she's cuter(;
Jorge	Don't know you guys but Myra is right ^^^^ Hahaha
Myra	I'm always right (; haha
Jorge	Woah... Let's not get too cocky here. Haha.
Myra	Confident (: Haha
Hazel	theres a difference :) haha
Jorge	Yeah but always? Haha. Why does the wind blow? Haha
Myra	Cause god(:
Kristine	all you guys are pathetic. mariphel did nothing wrong in this situation and hasnt said anything till HE texted her. if all you guys have so much hatred towards mariphel say it to her fucking face not over some stupid ass status that only a douchebagthats says "people are annoying who start drama on faceboooktumblr twitter instagram" so all you bitches have a fantatsic fucking day :) #lates
Hazel	hahahahaha well...#NOBODYFUCKINGASKEDYOU
Kristine	&when the fuck were you asked cause not one of these comments were directed towards you gurl. #fuckoff ;)

Franklin	hahaha look who talking. ur the one saying shit over facebook! LAWLZ
Hazel	Lol little bitch BIG mouth, the usual
Janelle	Franklin wtf do you think your status is ? Shit talking on fb ? Hmm weird.
Franklin	Hahaha this whole status was a joke cuz of what your little bestfriend said on hers. Lolz
Kristine	yeah defending my INNOCENT friend. lollollollol look who posted the damn status LMFAO. &whats funny is you were just texting her saying how much you care about her #readthemessages Hazel STFU idont even know you nor was i fucking talking to you so bye!
Hazel	And the mouth just gets bigger. BUT UR STILL A LITTLE BITCH. Franklins my friend and imma say what ever i damn well fucking please :)
Janelle	Who let the fucking dogs out ?
Rico	Kids in this town go hard... Hahahahaha
Kristine	hahahahahahahahahahahahhahahahahahahahahhahaha hahahahahahahahahahahhaahahhahaahahha imma say wuteva the fuxiwuntcuz bang is muhgurl 4 lif3
Janelle	Who let the fucking dogs out ?
Hazel	Funny name bang. Im pretty sure that means TO FUCK. Hmm stay classy.
Kristine	hahahahhahahahahhhahahah bitch you dont even know how she got the nickname, she plays a sport. so again byeeeeee Hazel.
Hazel	bye :))
Kristine	text me sometime girl, we can grab lunch. :)
Hazel	Im down :)
Janelle	You guys .....I still wanna know....WHO LET THE DOGS OUT ?!
Hazel	Dunnno who let you out? Lol
Jimboy	Alright.. Franklin's a homie... Janelle's a homie... Kristines my lover... Hazel... WHO THE FUCK ARE YOU??? No one cares what ur ugly ass has to say... and bitch look in the Mirror before you start talking shit...
Kristine	hahahahahahahhahahahahahaai fucking love you jimboy

Hazel	LOL i have no problem with my self image. :) andi can give a shit what ur punk ass has to say. OOPS i mean....that hurt. u win
Janelle	HAHAHAHH Jimboy <33
Hazel	Hes a keeper Kristine.
Kristine	i know he is.
Kristine	Hazel
Hazel	thats me :)
Kristine	obvi bitch lol
Hazel	Lol this really makes me laugh :) like i said before little bitches BIG mouths thats all there is to it.
Kristine	im not very little hazel
Franklin	Jimboy. Come on. This whole thing is dumb.
Hazel	yupp cause im fat :) more to love :) only dogs like a bag of bones!
Hazel	from what i can see sweetie u probly weigh 100 pounds soakin wet.
Hazel	Cause im so fat. I forgot already, hahaha
Kristine	well thanks for calling skinnny girl.
Hazel	Welcome.
Janelle	Hazel mentioned dogs, she must have let them out ? Or am I wrong ? Id love to know who let the dogs out ?
Hazel	ask the Baja Men.
Kristine	janelle ill give the baja men a call then let you know
Hazel	Well as much as id LOVE to stay and chat im sick of blowing up Franklins status :) tootles.
Dante	hahahah! this whole convo made my day. andifuckin love u Jimboy, well said
Emerson	glad you're happy Franklin! all that matters. Lawls
Noli	Franklin your a stud forget all this Facebook shit obviously you know you made a mistake at least you know that
Shanti	This just entertained me... I like how Rico is in on this haha... idk what happened with you guys but I love mariphel and Franklin you were cool too I guess, gotta take my cousins friends side on this though , but I got hope you guys can just move on from this.

YOU DIDN'T JUST SAY THAT

Liza	**No need for revenge. Those who hurt you will eventually screw themselves up. And if you're lucky, God will let you watch.**
Drake	**Free porn on TV tonight. Victorias Secret Fashion show!**
Trey	**I like blowjobs, she can be my employer;)**
Drake	**They say it's better to give, but I don't give a fuck**
Jack	**I need to get my tubes tied already...**
Judy	**Tell me about it , you would think I would have learned my lesson after 10 kids and 35 abortions .**
Stacey	**iloveeeeeeee pussy**
Jaeco	**me too !!**
Stacey	**♥**
Dino	**I like cock**
Gaven	**im pretty sure my boyfriend just got me pregnant. he just put it in my butt so hard i blacked out. but it was worth it ;p**

Samantha	**fuckin with me, i'm fuckin with you ;)**

Jack	**Your not the same person that I knew a year and a half ago. D:**
Neil	**Just becuz I got a sex change?**

Drake	**First trip to porn shop. Won't be my last.**
Dario	**LMAO**
Chad	**wow**
Chad	**shahhahaha**
Gordon	**I remember my first time**
Terence	**hahaha**
Hank	**Heard you bought some leather pants with no rear and a fishnet body suit. By the way, if you come out of the closet, there will be more room for your new outfits....lol**
Bentley	**everytime^ hahahaa**

Drake	**Girls fuck with a guys mind, guys fuck with a girls heart**

Brittney	**lololololololololol YOUR FAKE**
Angela	**no im not**
Brittney	**your faker than a glass doll**
Angela	**your faker then my sisters boobs**
Brittney	**HAHAHAHAHHAHAH**
Angela	**HAHAHAHAHAHH YES**
Brittney	**your faker than my prosteticleg..**
Angela	**your faker then my prosthetic dick**
Brittney	**your faker than the orgasm i had last night. OOOOOOH TOP THAT BITCH**
Angela	**OOOOOOOOOOOOOOOOOH STFU I HATE YOU THIS FAKE CONVERSATION IS OFFICIALLY OVER**

Brittney	she so cool she gives head with her shades on

Dianne	Horny?
Miles	Ohhh babyy;)
David	NO -___-
Miles	Hahahahahahah!!!!! GOOD
Dianne	Oh come on! Im a fun texter haha ;)
David	You suck wiener at texting lol
Dianne	Nooooo I don't!!!! Liar!!!

Samantha	fuckfuckfuck
Bart	i know right?!
Melvin	I guess u hav a word stuck in ur head o_O
Samantha	I like the word fuck sorry hommie
Bart	I loveee that word ;) its the most meaningful one in my book.
Samantha	Feesuyrw
Melvin	Shit i aint complaining haha

Brittney	Your lips look so lonely, would they like to meet mine? ;)
Wayne	come over NOW
Brittney	:):)
Enchong	but theyve already met, and i think they got along nicely. :D
Wayne	pretty sure the only thing ull be kissing is my ass ^^^
Arman	this is funny
Brittney	What is?
Arman	your status duh silly
Brittney	Hahaha why thank you:)
Arman	teehee
Brittney	♥

Drake	**Girls are like condoms, they spend more time in your wallet than on your dick.**
Dimple	**Hahahahahha !**
Claudine	**U just made me make a :0 face**
Roger	**Boys are like bra's, they hookup behind your back.**
Tope	**damn that was good ^ hahahaha**
Drake	**No roger get out of here**
Miriam	**i have a bra that hooks in the front LOL good one miriam**
Drake	**HAH yoo so fahni**
Tope	**i walk around with a condom on my dick. LOL good one hamzy**
Drake	**My dick is a condom :O**
Tope	**oh…**
Zanjoe	**Dude if u have condoms in ur wallet they have potential of ripping =O fuck bitches get money**
Slater	**The reason why we hook up behind your back is because you spend more time in our wallets than on our dick ... Duh**
Drake	**They expire faster as well**
Slater	**That too lol**
Chad	**LMFAO**
Benedict	**finally something cool haha**

Brittney	**"Who the hell names hurricanes and why do they give them the least threatening names? If you see on the news that hurricane Erin is blowing through, you're like 'Pfft. Erin? I can take that slut'. But if it's like hurricane Dicksmasher is coming, you'd pack your bong and leave immediately!" hahah oh how i love highdeas.com**
Tony	**hurricane TONNNNNNNNNNNNNNY!**
Brittney	**"So Dad... Since you've decided to drug test me randomly, I've decided to shave my ass pubes with your razor randomly. Karmas a bitch." HAHAHAHAH i love my life**
McKenzie	**HAHAHAHAHAHAHAHAha:ahahahahahahahahahahaha**

Brittney	"If everyone blinked at the exact same time....would anyone know?" HAHAHAHAHHAHAHAHAHHAHAHAH
McKenzie	Woooooooow that's true though. I'm telling you, that website fucking blows my mind! Hahahaima get on it right now...the website that is ;)
Brittney	HAHAH im so bored.......
Tony	highdeas.com is amazing:D
Brittney	HAHA i know right!?
Rayden	i♥highDEAS.
Eli	probably the best website ever. it's so funny haha

Samantha	i hate when people don't know how to fucking type. IT'S REALLY NOT THAT FUCKING HARD TO ADD AN EXTRA LETTER stupid.

Albert	you tell em samantha
Brittney	wat r u tlkin bout
Samantha	i hate you Brittney ahahah♥
Brittney	i hte u 2 ♥
Samantha	gud♥
Colt	they know how to type right, they chose not to cause they think it makes them cooler. some how.
Brittney	hey u ;]
Samantha	omg stingray hickey♥
Brittney	HAHAHAHAH my life literally sucks...he's still blocked on Facebook by me...
Samantha	hahhaha that was by far the funniest thing i've had to comprehend with you..
Brittney	Hahahhahaha the worst and weirdest shit always happens to me -___-
Samantha	and it was always when i was with you and i was like........ why
Brittney	Haaha you're obviously just bad luck....
Samantha	for you ;)
Brittney	pretty much
Samantha	c u n t f a c e

Brittney	p e n i s b u t t
Samantha	a s s n t i t t i e s
Brittney	5 d o l l a s u c k y s u c k y ?
Samantha	6 d o l l a l i c k y l i c k y ?
Brittney	c a n i l i c k y l i c k y d e n s u c k y s u c k y ?
Samantha	i f w e c u d d l e n d f u c k l o t s
Skipper	ha thats funny , hahahahahahahhahahahahahahahahhaha lol
Brittney	what
Golda	grl wht u tlkn bt

Brittney	are you brave enough to let me see your peacock? dont be a chicken boy, stop actin' like a beeotchima peace out if you don't give me the pay off come on baby let me see what you're hiding underneath ;)

McKenzie	Hahahahhahahhahhaaahaahaha fuck you
Brittney	you like it
Mason	Wow!!!! Your thinking like a.....Nvmahahah
Sherry	Nice Brittney
Brittney	Its a song hahahaha
Sherry	I figured that. But you are still a young lady, try not to forget that please. Love you!
Brittney	hahahai wont! love you too :)
McKenzie	this is so old.............
McKenzie	i like it (;
McKenzie	YOU SEXY GURLLL

David	She said she got a boyfriend FUCK That clown

Lawrence	Well I have a fish.......... oh wait sorry I thought we were talking about things that didnt matter hahaha
Wilson	haha goldfish*
David	Lmao!
Lawrence	Actually it's a Gilbert fish hahaha
Wilson	hahahaha wth

Lawrence	**Do you not know what that is hahahaha**
Marsha	**If you say your boyfriends got beef tell him I aint scared of him im a fucking vegetarian Ahahahaa♥**
Wilson	**hahahah^^^^^^ n Lawrence noo i dontt**
Dwight	**and soccer has a goalie, doesnt mean u cant score. And basketball has defenders, but if ur game is good enough, doesnt mean you cant get it in. And golf has many players, doesnt mean you cant get a stroke or two in... I think you get the picture im painting here. If not, well, it involves you having sex with her anyways lmao good luck, sir!**
Lawrence	**It looks like a gold fish butt they have fat faces I bet you've seen them but I was just joking ha**
Wilson	**haha i know..but now i kknow what type of fish that iss ahaha**
Lawrence	**Oh okay ha**

Brittney	**Will someone PLEASE marry Tori on Facebook so she stops complaining? She's single and likes it in between the toes and into her ear. Alrighty.**

Natalie	**yu 4got da armpit tho**
Tori	**im dyinh**
Brittney	**o damm SHE LYKZ DA ARMPIT PENNIETRASHUN 2**
Natalie	**who doesnt.**
Ethan	**I did it**
Brittney	**o rly**
Ethan	**Yea, but she gotta confirm it**
Tori	**do i know you...........**
Brittney	**oh my god hahah**
Ethan	**Idfk**
Tori	**K BYE**
Ashley	**Meow**

Brittney	**I wanna live somewhere where it's acceptable to be naked all the time...that way I would have no weird tan lines and I'd actually be tan. I'm gonna find that place..**

Jeff	meow
Brittney	bark
Jeff	moo
Brittney	quack
Jeff	oink
Brittney	weesnaw
Jeff	you win, iquit
Brittney	♥hehe
Jeff	nothing tops weesnaw
Cory	go to nude beaches !
Brittney	theres creepy old men thereeprobss..
Chris	but theres still old creepy men haha..go in your backyard. or africa.

Brittney **Superlaps can literally choke on Mr. Larry's dick...I'm STILL tired**

Chase	what's a super lap?
Brittney	you have to go like behind the softball fields then do bleachers...........what the fuck
Kristina	dude that is HELL
Brittney	STRAIGHT UP
Kristina	I think my teacher made my class do it once. but without the bleachers.
Brittney	i have to do bleachers like every fucking week godammmmit
Kristina	seriously? fuuuuuck dude imsorry
Patrick	ahaha that shit was eaaaaasy
Brittney	uhhhhhhhhhhhsike
Patrick	hahanaa not even. Piece of cake! Literally...
Brittney	hahahahah my teacher was the one marking it I would a got caught hoe
Brittney	ishalll :) okaybbittchh.

Brittney **hii suck dick fat dick**

Brittney	-_____-

Chase	**Good you came to terms with that.**
Paul	**if this was coming from anyone else i would think their facebook got hacked....haha.**
Brittney	**WHAT THE HELL DOES TTHAT MEAN**
McKenzie	**It means youre a sluttywhore**
Brittney	**ihateyou......**
Ryan	**ha fuuuuucked!**
Brittney	**-_____-!!!!!!!!!**
Brittney	**HCKED**
Jake	**Sorry, but Shawn I literally LOL-ed at your post man! haha!**
Carla	**hhhhhhhhhhaaaaaaaaahhhhhhhhaaaaaaaaaa^^^**
Justin	**me too.**
Brittney	**hahahahhaBEST**

Brittney	**fist me**

Jace	**ahahgroody !!**
Chase	**lawl**
Brittney	**yummy**
Jace	**loose ass pussy ahahah**
Brittney	**mmm**
Brittney	**yummy ass pussy**
Brittney	**prefferably Dezi**
Dezi	**idont fuck with fisting anymore**
Brittney	**only black girls...?**
Dezi	**nah no fisting! after you see some blood from that shit it takes the appeal out of it**
Charles	**Sure**
Miriam	**ok**
Eli	**hahahahaha**
Jaypee	**Brittney!!!grossss, take this off. BTW, I'm so happy I don't have to buy a queen bed!!! Have you seen yerroom?!?**

Tim	**I'm a virgin.**

Jack	**Gonna fuck shit up with Max saturday! I've missed my hoe!**

Samantha	**guys are all fucking assholes, I don't give a fuck if you say you're different because every guy has proven me wrong, go fuck yourselves.**

Conan	**not true :O**
Luis	**yup, we all suck...**
Colt	**Not to be mean but you must be going for the douchebags**
Mae	**Seriously... They all are the same.**
Edward	**im not**
Gemima	**she didn't ask for any of you guys' input, she's just saying how she feels. don't argue with her on her own opinion on her own status.**
Vilma	**i love you so much baby ♥**
Anrum	**Jaded**
Samantha	**It has been all guys not just one. They're all sick fucks who don't care about feelings and if one of you are I don't care, I go for the guys I go for and expect better out of them it's not hard to respect the girl you like.**
Vilma	**lets run away together ♥??**
Chester	**I<3samantha smile :]**
Samantha	**were doing it vilmaboobookitty we can eat sticks of butter together♥ and it's not about you Chester.**
Samantha	**Message me back.**
Mason	**Samantha the guys you must be around are just assholes I guess. There are alot of really nice guys out there that are looking for beautiful women like yourself. Don't worry. There is a guy coming your way when you least expect it.**
Mason	**She won't find him. He will find her. It's weird but that always is the case.**

Linsey	**that awk moment when your in your bra and thong and your 10 year old brothers friend sees you... :O oops.**

Taylor	**smooooth**
Gemima	**the hot friend?♥**
Colt	**did his face light up>?**
Colt	**haha**
Linsey	**hahahaha, i know right taylor): i had earphones in so ididnt notice him. and YES gemima♥ the hotttt one. and Colt, yes..it was cute♥**
Brian	**lucky kid**
Kylie	**cr33p ^**
Brian	**HAH yes...**
Brian	**loljk**
Clint	**Omggg what did u tell himm?**
Linsey	**Thanks Brian. And ahahah kylie♥** **And Clint, I didn't say anything. I just ran into my room coz I didn't know what to say ahahah**
Joe	**Omg Linsey.. You do this to me all the time**
Stacey	**the hot one??**
Linsey	**Hahhaha Gemima asked that too♥** **But yesss! It was:)**
Stacey	**AHAHAHAHAAHHA. dyeing. Lvoeyou**
Linsey	**Hahahhahahah love you so much♥** **It was good seeing you last night babbbyy!**
Stacey	**ahahahahiknowwi wish iwouldvee seen you for longerr♥ but soon :)**
Linsey	**Yesss. We shall soon have a family meeting so you can talk to dad♥**
Stacey	**haahah it needs to happen ASAP. shaniaaa reunion ♥**
Linsey	**I was just listening to her yesterday and it made me think about youuu♥ I miss our lame ass music videos**

Stacey	**Dear boys; your dick isnt like pinocchio's nose. It won't get longer every time you lie. Sincerely, reality.**
Kaleb	**that's why you put manuer on it and water it down. Duhhh.**
Stacey	**youre dick isnt a plant ahahahah**
Kaleb	***your**

Stacey	whatevvvv, i know the difference between youre and your i just dgafhahha
Kaleb	hahainoticed.
Stacey	ahahshuutup! :)
Kaleb	[0:
Stacey	ahhaha what kindof smiley is that?
Kaleb	the dank kind.
Stacey	ferrrsuuuureree. (o:
Glenn	I think im in love with this haha
Stacey	ahahahahi try girl :)
Glenn	well u succeed:phahaha
Kaleb	damn.
Stacey	damn whaaat
Kaleb	Damn Tato' Chips.
Stacey	whhaat are you tslkingabout?
Kaleb	*talking. The world may never knowwwww.
Stacey	ahhaha stop correcting my spelling ahhhah! i cant type with accrillicshaha TELLME
Bert	WHAT IT DOESNT OMG!!!
Stacey	Newssfllasshhahah
Bert	hahaha thanks for ruining it for me!;)
Lamar	lol well mines not pinocchios nose but it is like subway lol its a foot long
Stacey	TMI bl000d hhhhahahahaha
Lamar	lol ok gangbanger
Stacey	GANGBANGER?!?! Is there something I missed? Hahahaha when did I become one of those...
Lamar	when you said and i quote ''TMI Bl000d''
Stacey	Hahahaha that makes me a gangbanger?! Ddaamnnahaha
Bobby	mines like half an inch hard
Stacey	Part Asian bob???
Bobby	No full black. Thats big huh
Lamar	LOL Bobby is hellafunny

Drake	This stomach ache needs to go away so I don't create a Hershey's Chocolate fountain in the middle of the gym

Julie	eww haha
Rihanna	Gross...ha but baking soda & water helps haha
Drake	I'd rather shit all over the floor than endure the taste of baking soda and water hahaha

---

Samantha	10 of course bff♥

Tony	awww you're so sweet ugly bff♥
Samantha	you're fucking ugly
Tony	you're fucking stupid
Samantha	suck my dick ugly

Samantha	SHUT UP BITCH, suck my dick you fuckin' bop you better swallow it.

Tony	what the hell is a bop? DIDN'T I JUST TELL YOU TO SHUT THE FUCK UP?!but instead you go and post shit on my wall!fuck you.
Samantha	like a fucking slut LIKE YOU. FUCK YOU AND SUCK MY DICK
Tony	umm no
Samantha	i hate you go chocke
Tony	ahahahhahaim about to go hit a bong just cuz you told me to♥
Samantha	fuck that
Samantha	class
Samantha	hit
Samantha	that

Iggy	went from being "in a relationship" to "single."

Nathaniel	Whhhaat??
Iggy	Yep I couldn't do the lyes
Nathaniel	Text me555-5555and we can talk
Iggy	U might want to text sydney more she's the one hurt by this

Nathaniel	I will. I hope your ok.
Miguel	Sorry buddy hope your doing alright!!
Colin	I GOT UR NUMBER BITCH!!!
Colin	YOU BETTER GET ON YOUR DIRTBIKE AND RIDE FAR BITCH BOY
Colin	You little punk ass. Spoiled little cock smoking.mother FUCKING disrespectful cum gulping MOTHER FUCKER...
Caden	is this kid serious or fucking around?^^
Nathaniel	I was asking Myself the same thing
Colin	THIS IS SYDNEYS BROTHER IN LAW SPEAKING..AND YES I AM SERIOUS ..AND IM NOT A FUCKING KID. IGGY I BETTER NOT SEE YOU AROUND MY DAUGHTER EVER AGAIN AND OUR FAMILY.....!!!!
Iggy	Shut up Colin mind ur own business
Elisa	I have spoken to Colin and this will not happen again, my apologies for the tirade above, some people are just very protective of their loved ones when something happens to hurt them, this is private and we would appreciate it as a family that this is kept off facebook
Janet	Sorry to hear that iggy...... things happen for a reason..... but they do have away of working out...... stay strong...
Marcus	Sorry dude. Happens to the best of us. Riding your dirt bike = clearing your head.
Dalton	Whos sydney?
Cooper	Hey Iggy if you need anything let me know! I can leave work whenever.
Precious	i love you cuzzzz !♥

Lino	I'm a dick. Fuckin sue me
Bailey	Bitch I'm a mac. Apple. Bite me. If I was a dick ur girl would suck me
Lino	Who the fuck are you?^^

FACEBOOK DRAMA

David	**Facebook, I mean Dramabook***

David	**When karma is right around the corner and all your bullshit catches up to you. #JustAmatterOfTime ;)**

Lulu	**oh& apparently Ara hacks my facebook and twitter you are PHYSCO, bitch geeeez.**

David	**Stop lulu please drama ain't the solution -__-**
Lulu	**being pregnant > shitting themselves & doing cocain .....good thing i havent done any of them :) & no David she's hacking everything of mine this is not drama this is a phycotic girl.**
Hilary	**Can we fight her?**
Morgan	**Think she is just mad ur a fucking trillion times hotter then her an better body an lot more sexy :) I go to school with her sher is dumb!**
David	**Well don't talk shit on here find her and fuck her up!**
David	**Be lowkey about your bizz lulu!!**
Lulu	**Hilary i love you ♥**
Miraflor	**Hilary, Love you!!♥ and like I said....got your back (;**
Hilary	**True homegirls right here^^**
Lulu	**your the best ♥ i wouldnt fuck you, you go harddd iv heard you bitch people out ;) & security flipped out !**
Ashanti	**Lulu, i understand where your coming from, its hard to stay calm when your dealing with dumb bitches but this is the type of situation where you need to get the fuck off facebook find that fukin hoe and rip her weave out. hahaha**
Miraflor	**I'm crazy....especially when people mess with my girls! So you know, haha I got you (:**

Lulu	she goes hardddd ;) and no sorry once she hacked my twitter and facebook read all my messages i draw the fucken line.
Hilary	"no one touches my weave!!!!!" huh Lulu ?(;
Lulu	hold my mothaaafucken weeve !!!
Ashanti	& my eurrrings
Ashanti	& my poooodle.
Hilary	HOLD!...my fuckin...taco mothafucka
Lulu	wait wait dont shit yo self gurl....oh i guess only ara knows that
Ashanti	damn whats that smell? did some one pull a ara? hhaahha
Hilary	Team blonde must rally on the hoe.
Destiny	I swear I told everybody this girl was bad news from the beginning
Lulu	musta been a shitty party ;) and Destiny you knew what was up…i tried to be nice, it was her friend that made up a rumor she got drugged and raped so that was her excuse for cheating on thomas, after that it all went down hill
Miraflor	She crapped on herself? You've gotta be kidding...what is she...3
Lulu	bitches cant hang when there "addicted" to coke i guess !
Morgan	Trust. She isn't worth it honestly your so much better she is jealouse of u I put money on that shit she has an ape face ahahahahaga
Morgan	Or the hills have eyes ahahaha
Lulu	hills have eyes, hahahahhahahahahaha
Morgan	I'm telling u ahahahahahahahha
Herbert	wait how did she hack your fb? thats like really hard hahaha
Destiny	I wish I could put Emojis on this i would put the poop one ahahahahahahahahhaahahahak I'm done
Lulu	JUST MADE MY NIGHT ♥& because she's physco and i didnt sign myself off her phone one day…
Herbert	wow thats the defination of crazy haha like who sits there and trys to hack someones fb?that shits wierd maybe shes seretly in love with you....
Lulu	well she did make up a rumor she ate me out, hahahahaha this bitch is a jokeeee.
Herbert	hahahaha ewww i really think you should watch your back she prob stalks you or something

Lulu	obviously -___- FMLLL. like why would it be necessary to start a rumor im pregnant out of absolutely no where...
Herbert	haha yeah that must be annoying im sure everyone is like blowing your phone up asking if its true screw girls that start pointless drama
Lulu	you have no idea... i went to practice thousands of text calls and notifications soooo annoying omg.
Herbert	god im soooo sorry :/ hopefully it will blow over im sure people relize its not true by now
Lulu	i dont think this will blow over too soon... but everyone knows shes a physco bitch so it will be okay
Herbert	well i will pray for you :) just never make the mistake of leaving your fb logged in again!
Lulu	aweee thankyouu ♥ and i know mistake learneddd :)
Herbert	your welcome :) good you cant chang what happeed but you can definatly learn from them!

Lulu	Ara I am not pregnant & your a pathetic no life bitch to start a rumor
Fiona	That is so messed up. Ha
Debbie	Atleast you didn't shit yourself like she did
Sheldon	^^^win!!
Faye	Your pregnant?
Faye	Hahaha jk :)
Fiona	And even if you WERE pregnant, that doesn't make you a hoe. It could happen to anyone.
Marivic	Lolll put her on blast. What a bitch
Avery	Lulu, as being your big sister i'm giving you helpful advice. Keep it classy please. We all know Rumors are stupid..no need to blast them all on facebook. It just starts up more drama and i doubt you wanna put yourself in that situation.
David	I wouldn't even let that bitch lick my asshole after I shit
Miraflor	Lulu I got your back (:
Braxton	Hahahahaha David ^^
Ashanti	Hahahahaga Debbie!!!! Lol

Ashanti	Let's be reasonable here tho... This bitch shits herself passes out drunk and hopped up on other drugs at jay's after doing god knows what to whoever crosses her path and she is gonna sit her skanky ass down and type this shit? You gotta be kidding me lol what has this world come too. Haha
Lulu	I'm sick of people texting me aking if I'm pregnant that's why it's up ... Honestly this chicks one to talk when she has one of thee worst reputations in ctown, she needs to mind her own business I'm not pregnant and it's pathetic she has to pull a rumor out of her ass to make herself feel better
Destiny	lol just tell her she got played by jake ahahahahahaha
Dorothy	That's not what Jake said... – Ara
Ashanti	Jake's too nice of a guy to say anything haha
Dorothy	I have the messages if you really don't believe me
Ashanti	Plus what guy is going to be like oh ya I just used you for your free vagina hahaha
Destiny	Lulu after everything that has happened between us I can still say that you are a gorgeous girl and that I know you can handle yourself,these girls are just going to keep on talking but its your job to keep that gorgeous smile planted on that beautiful face of yours ok? ♥
Doyle	Hahahahahahahahahahahahahahahaha and I love Jake
Ashanti	It not that I don't believe but I know Jake he's a nice guy but if a girl is gonna offer him sex he won't say no lol
Destiny	oh doesnt everybody^^^^^?♥
Destiny	ahahahaha i agree with Ashanti!!like X10
Ashanti	Thank you! Lol
Lulu	Destiny i fucking loveee you ♥your beautiful too no matter what we have gone through im glad to have you as a friend :) thankyou times a million!
Gustavo	Someone needs to get Kendra wooped
Dustin	dammmmnnnnnnn
Homer	fightinnn words lol
Lulu	im not gunna critisize the way she looks because im not that low of a person i judge people on their actions not looks and who she is as a person is ugly...
Debbie	I love Jake ♥

Hamish	so much hate in the world :/
Ashanti	Who doesn't love Jake lol :)
Weston	ay yo... i dont even know you... but you are like 10X hotter than she is... and like shes a hoe... she can suck it...
Leopold	I still believe your pregnant
Lexi	girls are so pathetic.
Nolan	I love watching the shit girls do keeps me entertained haha
Lowell	Damn!!! This is intense. I give you major props for handling your business
Lulu	Leopold really !? Have you looked at the person who spread the shit about me she has by far more issues than I do
Leopold	I stand stiff...just like that guy did when he got you pregnant
Lulu	im not pregnant for the millionth time k.

Lulu	well now that everyone knows im not pregnant im going to bed, hahahahaha nightt.

Rodulf	Did you comeback with something better to her ? Hah
Lulu	she shits her pants at partys.... thats by far worse oh and does cocaine so i dont need a good come back hahahahahaha
Rodulf	Damn umm can I tweet this haha your comeback was .... "Your Ara smh" haha
Lulu	yes and write #team Lulu ♥
Rodulf	I shakl
Lulu	what your username?
David	HELLA drama lol
Dirk	Fake pregancy, cocaine, and shitting pants... Damn hahaha
Julian	whoah whoah whoah...... she shit herself and is talking shit... how ironic lol
Lulu	i dont care this chick needs to learn not to scew with me, hahaha text me David......and yes so you do the math and realize who the crazy one is
Dirk	She probably was doing coke while talking shit :P

Samantha	you can't have fucking everybody, choose one boy and fucking stick to him stupid slut.
Lester	Excuse you miss, but may i ask. Have you already chosen your boy?♥
Brittney	like
Tasha	Yes I can
Samantha	cheating wise tasha not flirting ;) hah and no love brittney. Lester I'm mad at you cause you won't let me give you a fucking birthday present♥
Lester	I honestly do not want anything♥!
Brittney	love love love ♥
Samatha	You should it's your fucking birthday LOVE. Sluts are literally pathetic just saying A(/!:?.88:;$:$;$:$&/"@/)28
Lester	Well i dont know, k! haha(:
Brittney	I Love Being a Slut
Samantha	yes we know Brittney
Brittney	;)
Mark	Cheaters never prospure
Samantha	remember when I texted you Lester over and over and froze your phone♥ ahh
Brittney	HAHAHAHAHAH that was so fucking funny.....
Lester	I dont remember that. hahaha :P
Samantha	Are you being sarcastic ? Because I thought it was really funny acually....
Brittney	Lester you didn't know...no it was actualllyy really funny
Samantha	You were not there lester it was after something ;) lallalala why am I perfect
Brittney	;) ;)
Samantha	you got so mad at me aahah and it was like all the way to your house and I was trying so hard not to laugh hahahaudhevvekssg
Brittney	Hhahahahahah because we were in the car with my mom....
Brittney	CAN YOU PLEASE COME OVER SOON SO WE CAN CAUSE MICHEIF AGAIN
Lester	Hahahahahh

Samantha	COURSE lots of trouble drinking beer smoking spice agahah and she got mad :(
Brittney	Ahhh we were such good children ♥ that was so long ago omg
Samantha	Like a year ago ahha. Sad!

Samantha	I don't understand how your "friend" could go after somebody that you like, or have had a past with and think it's completely fucking okay.
Rowena	agreeed.
Samantha	ahah love our lives

| Linsey | done acknowledging rumors and the people who spread them. :) |
| Nelson | pssstt did you know your done acknowledging people who spread rumors? |

Kynsley	i used to think you took my breath away, then i realized i was just suffocated by your bullshit. i'm seriously considering becoming anti-social from seeing how fucked up people are in this city. Fuck you all.
Stacey	what happpened kynsley?
Daniel	Yes what happened kynsley
Kynsley	no one gives a fuck about anyone anymore nowadays and it's the saddest thing i've ever seen.
Daniel	Very true
Kynsley	really though, i fucking hate everyone. words don't mean shit if your actions contradict.

| Tori | that bitch deleted the wallpost. Wahhhhh |

Kynsley	we we're straight killing her. what a skitchhh, like you just got caught up in your own lies girl. how do you feeeel. go call the rest of the world baby, but just be friends with them? nawmmsaynn(;
Tori	I hate girls. they such bitchezzzzzzzzzzzzz
Kynsley	i'm seriously going to be anti-social just by seeing how fucked up people are nowadays.
Tori	me too. i posted a status and im really annoyed holyshit im getting off facebook im dying bye
Kynsley	text me, love you ♥
Stacey	WHOM OMHG I WNANAN KILL SOMEONE TO

Kynsley	gotta get better with time, relationships should never rewind, betta leave it all behind, does that mean you could ever be minee.

Kynsley	sometimes, no matter how much you like someone. their just not good for you.

Kailyn	LOL 'cause I wear high heels to school I'm a slut... makes sense!
Helena	people are dumb.
Kailyn	I know right? haha, I don't remember ever doing anything to make people think I'm a slut, but the shoes def prove I am ♥
Norman	well obviously
Jerome	you might as well let your nuts hangout too you dirty slut♥
Norman	slut
Rainier	Jesus.. your not gettig my point
Kailyn	OKAY RAINIER, My name is Kailyn, and I am a filthy whore.
Estevan	No people call u a slut because u present urself that way
Jerome	hahaha swag
Rainier	See now we found the problem…let's make a plan on how to fix it

Kailyn	yeah? 'cause I can count the guys I've KISSED on one hand? Or becase I've never met you in my life? MAKES SENse. Clearly you know all about me
Rainier	In your face bro
Estevan	I was just sayn thats what people probaly see remember u judge people like peope judge you
Rainier	It's too late for that comment.. dick
Jerome	i cant count the number of bitches on my dick right now with 5 hands..
Kimberly	hi shut up Estevan, whoever you are. Kailyn is a buttercup blossom and doesn't need to be talked to like that. now go smoke some weed n calm the fuck down.
Kailyn	If you think I carry myself like a whore, why do you always try to hit me up on here?
Rainier	Fuck.. cold bloooddedd
Jerome	cant be seen by enemy uavs...
Estevan	I was just makeing a comment isnt that why peope post shit on here for likes and comments if u dont like me block me
Kimberly	lets beat him up lolololol
Rainier	Game over little bitch
Rainier	No Facebook wasn't made for that.. its made for FRIENDS! It's the key word..
Kailyn	Well I didn't have a problem with you until just now.... when you said I carry myself like a whore. When I've never even met you. I don't need to block you to prove that your a dickhead, you've already done that
Kimberly	IM A SLUT BECAUSE I WEAR THE COLOR YELLOW
Estevan	I didnt say u were a whore you are what u surrond urself with
Rainier	I'm a slut cause I let my thing hang out
Jerome	estevan...your just makin it worse..
Rainier	so you just said she's a whore... Your fucked up fool.. why are you such a dick
Kailyn	I'm a whore because I surround myself with whores then.... who are these whores I surround myself with that you know?
Rainier	Asshole.
Kimberly	I'm a slut because cheese tastes good on my pizza
Kailyn	I'm a slut cause I like cats

Rainier	I'm a slut cause I have a Facebook
Kimberly	Kailyn I think you're a slut, say something
Joyce	SO.. what you're tellin me is.. EVERY GIRL AT HOMECOMING is a slut cause they wore heels to school?!
Kailyn	yep!
Kimberly	I just got sum new heels, they're cute
Kailyn	oh didja?
Rainier	Deff
Joyce	Judgmental fucks. -_____-
	I ♥ YOU AND YOUR HEELS!
Andrew	HMU #butonlyifyourewearingheelsdoe
Kailyn	hittin' ya up now (;
Araceli	there just hatin cuz you can pull them off and actually walk in em (:
Alejandro	she' not a whore! she's a NICE LADY!(with good taste in shoes)
Brittney	cryin
Javier	SexyLovelyUniqueTantalyzing. swag.

Kailyn	When a weird ass kid you've never met asks you out, but you say no so he tries to make you feel bad by saying he's been dumped 37 times.........

Jacob	GET AT IT GURL
Kailyn	RIGHT? Obvi h3z @ k33pEr d03.
Colt	Wanna go out
Kailyn	duhh, datz why i be helluh lewkin fo a boyfran yhu knoe
Colt	I've been dumped 169 times this month though
Kailyn	pity datez fo dayz
Colt	Fer dayz n166a
Rainier	Why are you so mean to me
Kailyn	"yeah... but honestly, i'll be lucky to live to be 25 or so..." "why?" " i have depression issues to the point it makes me physically ill"
Rainier	Ima go kill myself now cool..

Kailyn	i apologize for puttin yo ass on blast
Rainier	X_x
Kailyn	"oh?:/" "yeah I write songs to keep y mind off it all"
Brittney	hes iming me asking if im single and i told him im bi with a gf and he asked if im in an open relationship and he wants to get to know me in person
Kailyn	that's how it started! I told him I was a lesbian for females and cats only and that I didn't like human boys and he STILL tried
Rainier	Sorry didn't realize you were going to put me on blast

---

Kynsley	If you're absent during my struggle don't expect to be present during my success.

Kailyn	If everyone on Facebook hates everyone else on facebook like they say they do, why do we all still go on it......
Leonard	because we're constantly bored:)
Edwin	cuz we all ♥ drama :) hahahahahahahah
Kailyn	Why don't we all play some Mario kart or something then.... Thats more fun than facebook!
Kailyn	And I think Edwins right haha, all people do on here is start drama and talk about how much they hate drama... Hahaha
Edwin	if you wanna have a popular status or wall post, just post something completely meaningless that sounds philosophical and you most likely will get a bunch of likes or comments, its kinda sad how its changed
Kailyn	Right?! Or just post something bashing someone else to make yourself look badass. So annoying!
Calvin	smoke weed and play mario kart...

Jack	It shows how muh of a person you are when you try and appologise for something and you try to talk it out. and they just fucking dont care. And they were the people that made a huge deal about it. well guess what bitch. your not the best, stop actig

like your the shit. cause thats fucked up. There are people who know alot more than you and have been in the scene longer and they just think your pathetic. oh and if you havent noticed, your boyfriend is kinda a flamer. ♥

Wendy	**uhm i'm pretty much going through this exact same shit**
Monica	**You kids crack me up ♥**

Brittney	**Goin to da cyber pooolice....me andKailynDUN GOOFED UP!!**

Lexi	**ohhh god hahahahahah.**
Brittney	**Hhahahahah ♥**
Rainier	**Kewl..**

Camille	**F . U . C . K . Y . O . U . ((:**

Keegan	**Ha**
Camille	**Whaat ?**
Bonnie	**K.**
Camille	**Never you love ((:**
Keegan	**who r u talkin about?**
Bonnie	**♥ THAT'S WHAT I THOUGHT!**
Camille	**Love you ((:**

Jack	**I have a serious fucking question...WHAT IS UP WITH PEOPLE'S BULLSHIT.**

Vice	**iknorite?**
Monica	**Growing up ? duh.**
Jack	**No. Like just everyone is all uptight now. I'm like leave me alone.**
Monica	**Try deleting all the people in your life that cause drama?**
Jack	**It's not even just friends. It's like all adults now. Like honestly... I don't give a fuck anymore.**

Monica	I don't wanna be the bitch to say this but, from my past iv'e concluded that one day your going to just have to say fuck the bullshit and grow up. In thess means "being a normal person of society" Which is utter fucking shit. If i had a choice id still have all my peircings,sweet hair and all that good shit.
Jack	I will never be "normal" Aha. I just can't. I've been trying but people just are so uptight like if i make 1 little mistake, they get so mad at me!
Monica	thats people for ya,
Jack	I hate people ♥
Monica	me too
Dinah	tight assholes.
Yvonne	sometimes you just need to get away from it all turn your phone off and go to disneyland and go on screaming and scream it out
Jack	I just wanna cry!
Yvonne	crying feels good too but those are things you shouldnt devolge with people

---

David	Like my status if you wanna get out of this town because low lifes, druggies, thiefs, sluts, and assholes annoy you.
Anthony	AMEN!
Rhea	anyone who likes this status is lying cause everyone who says their gonna get out never doesss
Rafael	Hahaha this town probably has the fewest of all of those bro!
David	No man trust me their all spoiled losers
Anthony	im not lying. im out this bitch ASAP hahah
Rhea	^ the theft part maybe the fewest but i dont think you know this town if you say that theirs nothin else to do here so why not get fucked up and be a little slut
David	Let me come(:
Darius	and me!
Rafael	Haha you guys wouldnt last a day were i come from, after a week in my hometown you'd be wishing you could be back in your sweet little ol' town! (and no im not that kid thats like

	"oh im from the ghetto i go through all types of stuff you dont even know" cuz i hate kids that try to brag about bein from the hood, real people from the gutter dont glorify the hood, they hate it.)
Darius	i know ill go to the beach house with you two!
Rhea	haha im not sayin that i lived in LA. my friend got shot on my street walking out of church so we moved. im just sayin there are little sluts and druggies thinking their the shit starting drama
David	Down!
David	So true rhea
Rafael	Exactly, starting drama, drama aint shit except to drama queens, there isnt drama started where i come from. You guys should be gratefull you live in this town! No gangs, poverty, murder.
Rhea	?? ha well wherever your from im pretty sure i understand you shouldnt say people dont know where your coming from when you dont know someone elses life and no im not grateful to live here cause behind all the gangs poverty and murders at least theres real ass people there
David	Raf - San Diego isn't that ghetto tho man. I used to live their. It has it's parts but yeah their is very few murders. The people are old school and real wit it tho.
Sandra	I love this Town.
Wade	You think you have it bad come to my State
Alastair	i don't see why people get so butt hurt about this topic. This town isn't a bad place, maybe you need to just stop worrying about it and the people that do bad things, it doesn't bother me because i don't have time to worry about those people. those are the choices they make so just let it be, oh and if you really want to get out of this town, go right ahead.
Santino	ull find all that shit anywhere u go hawmie
Jewel	I hate this town because you need a car to function and the bus system is retarted. old people working at jobs who are for the youth. im so over it here
Rafael	@Rhea~ thats true im sorry i shouldnt be assuming things, and yeah the realest people are from the hood. @David~

	hahaha im not from SD, im from Stockton look it up bro crazy shit makes SD look like heaven lol.
Zenith	Every place you go to though is going to have all the same kinds of people we have here..
Jaser	Im glad i got out of that town, right now im in the Bay area and its chill but idaho lots of drama
Danica	So when are you moving?
David	Uh your wack get out of here with that hatin bs you dont even know me
Jefferson	lets go to CANADA!! all they got is bears n shit:D

Samantha	in the end someone will always get fucked over, because nobody knows how to commit to their feelings.

Donnel	stop being depressed </3
Samantha	i'm not, it's just shit you realize hahaha i promise im happy :)
Donnel	okay, you better be ♥
Samantha	i am lovely♥
Jestone	Thats the truth ;p Omg this is perfect for what im going through right now thank you for posting this hun
Donnel	^^^ this guy knows everyone I know... and I have no clue who he is. awkward.
Jestone	Sorry what can i say i know the real people and theres probably a reason i dont know you
Mason	I beg to differ
Jestone	easy kid let the men talk...
Mason	Um the only men in this room are probably me and maybe you. I'm not gonna judge past what I am, but coming off like that makes you that much less of a man. But i was begging to differ with samanthas status.
Jestone	My mistake i thought you were bein a lil smart ass
Mason	Good man right there. Chose not to argue. Saw that it was a simple misunderstanding.
Jestone	Im not an asshole i can admit when i make a mistake. i appologyze nothin against you it just seems like every time i

	comment on Samanthas status someones always is talkin shit on me and i dont even know these pricks
Mason	Yeah well the world is full of ignorant people. People just need to learn to have some appreciation in this world and show some caring in life cause if the world came to an end and it was you and the one person would you continue to act the way you do or are you gonna try and become friends and survive. We live once and there's toomuch sadness and hurtful people in this world. It needs to be changed
Jestone	I agree well said
Donnel	Jestone: it's cute how you assume I'm not "real". I said nothing offensive to you, and you came off as a stuck up asshole who acted like he knew someone he didn't know the first thing about, and you call that real? How bout we start over, Hey, I'm Donnel, nice to meet you.
Samantha	What the hell
Mason	^^^ hahaha samantha we need to hang out!
Samantha	Nooo
Mason	Ouch that hurt.
Jestone	Donnel I understand what you meen man but look at the comment... I never said u arent a real person, I said theres probably a reason I dont know you... Put the guns down fool Im not ur enemy unless u want it that way. Everyone I meet gets a certain amount of respect from me and it grows or decreases from what they do or say. so if u wanna take this back to square one im fine with it.

Jack	So... she's just the drug dealer now? Not my best friend anymore. Her and her new best friend just clicked, and i'm never around? No bitch, I'm never around cause you always blow me off. "once your off grounding and you have money hmu and we can smoke" Your best friend doesn't say that. There supposed to say "Oh well when your not grounded let's hang out." Whatever. I'm done. Have a great time with him, and his friends and your boyfriend. I'm done thinking we are best friends. This year and a half was all a lie. I wish 3/10/11 never happened. :/

Ethel	**Fuck bitches and get money!**
Yvette	**friends come and go and people change, learn not to get attached or youll learn the hard way ♥**
Jack	**She was my best friend. Honestly every day we would hang out. If we didn't hang out we would skype. From day 1 we were best friends. I miss her so much. So fucking much. I've tried talking to her. she's like "you're being over dramatic bla bla bla". Whatever.**
Yvette	**i feel you dude , i lost my best friend like that. It's not meant to be thats why having a "best" friend is stupid cause people change and have different interests so they grow apart its normal. when i quit doing shit a lot my friends didnt know how to relate to me, its just part of life. ♥**
Czarina	**never forgive someone like that.**
Jack	**^you know who this is about right?**
Czarina	**i think i have an ideaaa.**
Jack	**Yeah.. But you saw this comming right? I know I did.**
Czarina	**a little i guess. i never really got good vibes from her to begin with. ;o**
Martin	**<<<agrrees with czarina**
Jack	**I'm finally realizing all the hurt that I got put through cause of our "friendship"**
Jack	**And she dumpedDolphyfor this new kid. Wow. Shows how great of a person she is.**
Czarina	**let her do what she wants. it's her reputation getting ruined.**
Gerry	**I'm sorry :(**
Jack	**It's o.k.**
Gerry	**:/**

Nadine	**Thanks for pretending to be my friend and care. I've told you so much cuz I thought I could trust you but instead you decided to be a back stabber and two faced. You lied right to my face. The truth is, yes, you're pretty and yes, you know it. Stop thinking you can solve everybodys problems cuz you cant, you just like the drama. I can see right through you now and what you did really hurt me, so im done, you win. Also, to someone else, please stop**

trying to ruin and take my friends away from me. During spring break I'm going to Idaho then my cousin is coming and that's all I'm doing so please stop putting words in my mouth. I'm done with everybody. </3

Ricardo	Love you Nadine! Cant wait to see you!
Nadine	Love you too! Cant wait to come, you have no idea!!
Paolo	Nadine ♥
Nadine	Paolo ♥
Paolo	haha idk why i randomly commented, but i miss youuu.
Nadine	I miss you tooooooo!
Meredith	youuu okaaay Nadine?
Nadine	im writing you a note right now, i'll give it to you tomorrow!
Meredith	isss it explaining why youure upset?
Hubert	dont be mad, be glad XD
Nadine	yep, in full detail haha
Nadine	hahah that just made me smile Hubert! haha
Quincy	You are going to see Ricardo?!
Meredith	is it about....... the chick i wrote to you about?
Hubert	well then my job here is done :P
Nadine	Quincy - yesss, i am(:Meredith - the first part of my status is about her yes! Hubert - well thank you :))
Meredith	OHHH SHHHHHHOOOOOT.
Quincy	when?!
Shelly	Love you baby ♥
Paulette	I havent talked to you in forever, but keep your head up. Everything will work out !(:
Carmen	HAHAHAHAHAHA OMG I FRICKIN LOVE YOU<3333
Mercedes	Nadine i love you and ill always be here for you!!! Text me if you neeed anything

SEX, DRUGS & ALCOHOL

Jack	**Eat acid. See God.**
Candace	**AMEN.♥**
Jack	**I'm frying face.**
Candace	**lucky. how the fuck are you on FB?**
	shit was difficult for me. but then again, i took 5 tabs for my
	first time. double dropped too.
Jack	**Ohhh myyyy god! the screen is like warpping.**
Candace	**good! be impressed~http://www.youtube.com/**
	watch?v=yzC4hFK5P3g&ob=av3e
Neil	**I smoke it**
Carson	**i can stand behind that this one**
Carson	**omg if i saw that video on fry........**
Neil	**try the peepsbeeps app…LMAO frying at a party or concert**
Candace	**<3 peeps beeps hottie alert & freaking people out with the**
	popo sirens
Neil	**<3 the horns to make people gtfo of my way … Jack youd like**
	the hot dudes horn

Jeffrey	**you stoner, lets kick it soonsies.**
Jack	**Can we do acid?**
Gerry	**Only if I get one! :)**
Jeffery	**Txt me you sluuuu**

Megan	**if anyone needs heroine hit me up. 1800uglydruggybitch.**
Vladimir	**im callin you right now is it dank?**
Liela	**AHHAHHAHAHHAHHAHHAHHAHHAHAHAHAHAHA**
	HHAHAHHAHAHAHHAHAHHAHA

Brittney	**There are only 3 things a girl needs: love to make her weak, alcohol to make her strong, and best friends to pick her up when both things make her hit the floor.**
Charles	**Alcohol to make her strong? the only thing I've seen alcohol do to women is make them take off their clothes**
Brittney	**Oh.........................?**
Rizza	**toushe! this is true.**
Chester	**i hate love....**
Brittney	**Why"?**
Chester	**:/**

Jack	**All I really want is some Jack and Coke. ♥**
Gerry	**Eww**
Phoebe	**Skip the coke please just ice**

David	**Sex is the cure to my insomnia. I need a girlfriend and she needs to share a room with me cuz this is not okay haha**
Raffy	**How bout a j?**
David	**Sex> weed**
Raffy	**Or both at the same time**
David	**Sex then weed then sleep.(:**
Shania	**Sex weed eat sex sleep**
Felicity	**lmao**

Brittney	**Samanthaaa. HONESTLY, we've had our differences in the past, and there was a really long time where we had a lot of tension between us, but I'm really glad that we somewhat fixed things. I respect you a lot as a person, and I miss hanging out with you like we used to. You need to keep your chin up and smile BECAUSEE you're beautiful and some sexy boy is gonna come and swooop**

your ass up soon I knowww it♥ I hope you're doing well, and like I said before, I'm here for you if you ever need anything. :)

Samantha	awe honestly same goes for you ♥ i miss freshman year and when you took my smoking and drinking virginity hahah okay bye :)
Brittney	HAHAHAHAH omg I seriously corrupted you...when I was talking to the frog...
Samantha	shut up bitch ahhaha. and your mom was like you guys are high..and then i burned you and i felt really bad inside but i wanted to laugh cause it was funny :(ahhaha
Brittney	Hahahaha when I was so high that I kept trying to light the mouthpiece ahahha...honestly it would have been funny if it didn't hurt so fucking bad
Samantha	hahahah and i kept laughing before i took a hit and i was like WHAT THE FUCK IS THIS ahh spice ♥ hahah and i know i like didnt know what to do ahhahaha
Brittney	HAHAHAH oh my god that night was just fucked up on so many levels...I had to put my hand in a bowl of water to stop me from crying. Spice is fucking stupid!! I smoked this weird kind of it and I was sitting there twitching and I only hit the bong once..like why..
Samantha	hahhahhha and the reality of it is that we just stayed home... and then we spent new years sober as a duck...hahahahah ew i think its meth.........
Brittney	Hahahah we had one beer and played dance central with my mom ♥ They dont even know what it is......
Samantha	hahhaha omg yeah♥ i wasnt good at that game...at all hahahah COOL thats scary.
Brittney	Hahahah I like the wii one better..its so fun..this new years betterr be fucking amazing hahaa. yeah it freaks me out i wanna go on a google mish and find out what spice is..
Samantha	whats google mish...♥ ahhaha and I SWEAR TO GOD IF I WATCH BOYS PLAY COD FOR 4 HOURS IM GOING TO CRY. ill probably see you drunk as fuck somewhere ;) hahaha.
Brittney	Like a google mission ♥ HAHAHAHHAHA that was honestly so fucking rediculous we missed the goddamn ball drop and

	NOBODY would pick us up...hahaha most likely I always see everyone when I'm drunk as fuck my life sucks
Samantha	hahahhaahha we litterally called everyone hahaha and we sent out that really ugly picture......♥ its otay i hate everyone and my life is aweseome
Brittney	Hahahhahhahah ew we called gross guy. That picture was honestly so fucking funny all of those pictures were but they were on my ipod which got stolen wah :(hahahah
Samantha	WOW TYPICAL BRITTNEY WHOD LOSE HER GOD DAMN IPOD jk♥? Hahah
Brittney	HAHAHAHHAH i lose fucking evvverything in my life. -__-

---

Jack	I need some LSD.
Jack	No... Really. Who has tabs?
Jack	^Absolutly not. :d
Melanie	you just never shut up about your fucking drugs
Jack	^^cocaine -giggles like a scene girl-
Gerry	LOL. Well hello? ;)

Drake	90% of you look like your bound to rehab after highschool for alcoholism
Benedict	just cuz all of us drink doesnt mean were going to end up being some population of haggard ass bums.
Ruby	Haggard ass bums start off like Benedict.
Benedict	shiiiit so what i like iit
Irish	yeee

Samantha	Holy shit you looked fucked uppp! So many fucking people I missed the fuck out :(

Vilma	**I know shiiiit so faded i think i might quit since im addicted to crystal meth now, sorry forgot to tell you. ♥ Look at all those people and who's leg is in front of my face?! Holy tits**
Samantha	**Nope you told me when we were doing it...♥ who the fuck is that flexible oh my god?!?! Do you see that douche getting head!!??!:$2?:$2 trashy**
Vilma	**Wow who the fuck got a rimjob on my bed..... Good thing I washed my sheets. Oh yeah sorry forgot we shoot up in McDonald's every morning together**
Samantha	**mickey dees is how the fuck we do it. Omggg is that Justin beiber?! How the fuck.. Damn**
Vilma	**I hate him who the fuck invited him?**
Samantha	**probably some litle bitch**
Vilma	**Definitely a head giving whore.**
Samantha	**yupppppp like all of our town...great place to shop with people you know ;)**

Drake	**Dear facebook, no one cares about pictures of you getting faded**

Jack	**When ever someone asks me a question...my answer will be "Just go smoke a bowl" ♥**

Karen	**HAHAHA, DAMN RIGHT♥**
Jack	**Karen! :D**
Karen	**Jack!! o:**
Jack	**I'm hungry. Bring me a baked potato.**
Karen	**Yer Too Far, Jack. D: And I Am Hungry Too, I Have A Bunch Of Potatoes, But I Dont Know How To Cook Em. XDDD**
Karen	**Hmmmm.. Too Lazy. o.o**
Jack	**Go to culinary school**
Karen	**Im Too Lazy For That Jack. D:**
Karen	**Hahaha.**
Jack	**Smoking pot makes you fat.**
Karen	**I Know Right? XDD I Ate Del Taco After I Smoked A Bunch With Holly. o.o I Ate 2 Chipotle Burrito's. So Bomb. And**

	When I Eat, I Get Soooo Fat. D; Too Much Pot, Man, I Swear. >.<
Jack	Omg. I went to Dennys like on sunday cause I was so fucking baked. And like I felt like the guy knew I was high. But I felt so fat. I am getting fat. EWE!
Karen	That Sounds Like The SHIT! Hahaha, Denny's Baked.. I Wanna Try It XD
Jack	My Mom Knew When I Came Home Last Night That I Was Stoned.. It Was So Gay... Like... As Soon As I Stepped Into The Door, I Looked At Them For 5 Seconds, And My Eyes Get VERY VERY VERY Red, Sooo... She Saw My Eyes For A Split Second... And I Ran Into The Bathroom Because I Had To Pee... So I Took A Shower To Make Sure I Sober Up A Bit And So I Can Wake Up... And So My Eyes Wont Be So Red When I Got Out... So... I Went To Take A Shower... And I Decided.. My Stoner Ass Decided... To Lay A Towel On The Ground, And Sleep XD
Jack	How much trouble are you in?
Karen	Im Not In Any Trouble. HAHAHAHA. FTW♥
Jack	:D
Marjorie	I Like My House Because I Can Smoke All I Want And Not Be In Trouble XD
Rowley	ive lost like 30 lbs since smoking

Samantha	fuck that class, and hit that bong.

Jason	fuck that class, and hit that bong.
Samantha	wolfgang
Jason	wat??? Hahaha
Samantha	how dont you know...
Jason	wat does that mean?? please tell
Samantha	its a fucking rap grouppppp.
Jason	ow hahaha
Samantha	k
Jason	why did u randomly say that?

Samantha	**when all people talk about is how fucked up they get every weekend hahah oh.**
Jomer	**ha not you**
Samantha	**I'm pure as fuck.**
Jomer	**ha the pure life for life**
Samantha	**duh :)**
Jomer	**got to love your grandma**
Jobim	**people for you in this town**
Samantha	**Pretty fuckng much ha**
Irene	**ohhmyygodd this is my first partyyy im so fucked up im only 12 years old♥**
Samantha	**My moms calling omggg I feel sick I coughed out a bowl omg ♥**

Linsey	**the nights you can't remember with the people you'll never forget ♥**
David	**♥**
Linsey	**Last niight was amazing ♥**
David	**yeah it was (; i had fun. idk bout you**
Linsey	**I didd have fun boo :) even thoo I can't really remember...but like its all starting to come back to me gradually**
David	**haha yeah i cant believe i drove home after that....**
Linsey	**That was so dangerous baby :(after you left I was worried af about youu.**
Kylie	**dont drive underrr the influenceee silllys!**
David	**i was okay tho♥hahaha**
Kylie	**Still! Next timee call someone, better safe then sorrrrry(:**
Kristian	**stupid**
David	**faggit^**
Kristian	**oh ya^..**
David	**your a punk. get off my girls status and yeah**
Kristian	**and yeah? youre talking about driving drunk. faggit.**
David	**fight me**
Kristian	**kill some wife/mother on the road. thats not cool putting yourself in that position**

Linsey	you arent cool Kristian.
David	go suck another mans dick and I wasnt drunk u queer so gtfo and go make some friends or something
Kristian	never said iwas... really mature kid...
Linsey	idont even kno you Kristian. kbye.
	and David is very mature♥
David	little kid i can control myself. and Kristian like i said, go make some friends ♥ you babeee
Kristian	your promoting your bf to be an idiot... go put yourself and others in harm then fuckin talk about it. mature..
Linsey	♥ you too booo
Kylie	Kaaaaay, just saying; you guys are cute, how you defend eachother and stufffff aww
David	you sound like my mom or something. beat it kid
Linsey	i adore you Kylie♥
Kristian	your mom? nah just some1 who doesn't wanna see some kid or mom get into an accident because of idiots. Cya
Kylie	Awhh I adoreee you toooo♥ But no driving uti kiddos, call me!(:
David	thanks for you advice, im sorry you have no friends Kristian, it was 4 am and I wasnt drunk Kylie. (:
Kristian	welcome...and oh ya no friends... good 1
Kylie	Oh oh kayy just checkinng♥
David	obviously not if your creepin on my girls page. Justsayinn
Linsey	Kristian really idk you kid, gtfo my status please.
Daniel	I'm not trying to cause drama, but Kristian has a point

---

Jack	That awkward moment when my mom said she's not going to tell my dad if I smoke weed. She's not o.k. with it. But she said she really can't do anything
Victoria	More like the awesome moment.

Brittney	One of my "friends" just said nevermind to hanging out with me because I refused to jack a bottle for them, HA! Fuck everyone seriously.

Jericho	woowww not a friend
Bruno	fucked up
Brittney	Obviously fucking not. I seriously hate all of my "friends"
Brittney	So done. I put up with way too much ha
Jericho	come hang out with me :))
Brittney	No riiiiiiiiiiide
Jericho	Grrrhaha
Pamela	not a real friend
Kaiden	id be sad too if ididnt have a bottle): hahaha but not somethin to be a dihkabboutanad not hang out with youhhahahhaa
Brittney	One of them told the guy to call me and that they would only pick me up if i jacked them a bottle and if i said no then to tell me nevermind. Like I have such shitty ass friends

---

Jack	Fryyuiiiinnngggf faccccve!!!!

Trey	like: how i saw you at kaiser today
Samantha	ollie definitely said "hes trying to get a meds for the wrong reason" hahahaha i laughed ♥
Trey	it was just benadryl! Haha
Samantha	benadryl is amazing as fuck, megan introduced me ♥
Trey	leeeeeeeean! and i only got a box of it so i can't do anything:(
Samantha	ahgahhah take all of them i got oxycodone today fucker♥
Trey	lucky motherfuck. lemme get sooome!
Samantha	maybeeeeeeeeeeeeeeeeee........♥
Trey	fuxya. you were very rude to me on halloween missy you owe me some;)
Samantha	fuck that night♥ ill bring some tomorrow hahah ♥
Trey	it was pretty gay cause i was in the trunk for the night<33
Samantha	i was really bitchy to everyone for no reason and i cried by myself but no one noticed i was crying hahahahah. BUT OKAY IL LBRING YOU SOME>♥
Trey	oh, well that sucks diiick:/ and tanks bb!
Samantha	you suck dick. so its all good. and course booboo!

Jack	**Going to bed. I feel like crap. I'm crying. Never doing that much shit in one day. Cause the next day i'm still fucked up. D:<**

Brittney	**Do I look like a fucking clinic?....do not ask me for weed I barely even smoke ahahah fuck you**

Greg	**Let me get some of that dankity dank guuuurrrlll**
Clark	**what kind of indicas do you recommend?**
Brittney	**ON DECK WITH PURPLE LLAMA ASS OG KUSH HMU**
Greg	**Sooo you got shrooms?.....**
Lester	**Whats a clinic ?**
Brittney	**Lester hi**
Lester	**No. Whats a clinic ???**
Brittney	**you dont know what a clinic is?..**
Lester	**I do not. Would you like to inform me... (:**
Brittney	**texxxxxxxtmee♥**
Lester	**No.... Tell mee!**
Brittney	**i will when you text me!**
Lester	**My phones dead and i cant find the charger..IM??**
Brittney	**okkkkkim me**

Jack	**vodka.and.monster.anyone.**

Divine	**Vodka straght and?im in**

Brittney	**Teenagers drink for the sole purpose of getting fucked up, and adults drink just because they fucking can..I want to drink just because I can....k**

Alwyn	**heroin**
Owen	**why drink when we can be Wall flowers?**
Brittney	**whats a wall flower.......**
Owen	**sober people at partys of drunks...**
Brittney	**hahahah fuck wallflowers**

Owen	or when people go to dance parties and dont dance but stand and watch people...
Brittney	i love watching people dance
Owen	do you own cats?
Brittney	no
Piyush	if ur not drinking to get fucked up there's no reason to drink... go hard or go home ahhaa
Brittney	if you think about it thats really really stupid...
Colby	i will drink cus i can get fucked up legally!!!!!!
Colby	sike
Owen	i drink because i like hang with hommies and have a goodtime. idont drink to the point where im being a sloppy fuck and no one is gonna let me hang because i annoyed everyone . :D
Brittney	that's true
Owen	I mean like last week.... some people werent meant to consume alcohol.....

Jack	Everything in the distance is morphing. And going in a counter-clockwise fashion. It's really fucking neat

---

Stacey	never drinking one sip of alcohol ever again. mark my fucking words.

Bryan	Woahhhhhbrah
Stacey	Most terrible thing ever aha
Bryan	Ha what happened that made you even decide that??
Stacey	Long story! But ill drink beer, beer doesn't count....Ahha Seriously though, I almost witnessed a death. No joke ha.
Trey	Stacey hahaha that's fucking funny af
Stacey	What is trey! Omg the f it shirt I just remembered that hahayayya ! :)
Trey	I'm never drinking alcohol! But I'll drink beer(; hahah I love you

Bryan	Ha makes perfect sense!:)
	I'm gonna be honest I'm super fucked upppha
Trey	I'll be honest I'm bored as hell
Stacey	Ahhaha beer is straight, its not that bad, when dranked responsibly! ;) ahah I'm kidding. Love you to mwuahah
Trey	Yeah foshizzle(: just don't die cause I'll miss you(;
Fritz	i feel ya have had that experience, if it's the experience i think it is. the smell of hard alcohol still makes me sick after 5 months;/
Stacey	No I didn't die, I was straight, my friend just was the most terrible I've ever seen anyone... And it just as easily couldve been me so I'm done ahaha
Eli	I haaaaate alcohol:(
Bryan	Ha some people just cant handle this Town?
Eli	some people just go way over the limit sometimes..
Fritz	yeah i didn't think it could happen to me. i think i had alcohol poising a little. but i'm kinda glad it happened because now i'm much more cautious
Stacey	Ahah yeah ferreal, I thought all that shit was a joke, but nope. Aha, I need to be so much more carefull.
Fritz	reality checks suck sometime ;P
	i'm out, hope your friend feels better
Althea	is she still ok?
Stacey	Thanks fritz, means a lot actually aha And ferreal, aha
	Yeah I'm textin her every 2.5 seconds althea aha, thanks for everything by the way you actually made me feel better aha
Althea	aww anytime...i was just worried i didnt want no one dying yano
Stacey	Ahahferreal me either, I was freaking the fuck out, aha thanks girl aha!
Althea	haha anytime...and im soo glad u and shithead are back!!
Stacey	Hahaah me too! :)
Roman	thats a lie lol

Jack	Not going to kandieland anymore. I almost got arrested. For weed alcohol. a pipe and ciggs. and being under the influence. Idk when

I'll be able to rave again. Or go to shows. Or hang out with friends. I fucked up and lost my parents trust. D: I'm really upset with myself.

Stacey   when I'm high I realize how fucking stupid every single commercial on tv is. theyre annoying bahah

Fritz   more like how stupid so much shit is. but those ones are stupid because they're targeted towards people that are out of school at home for them to do shit, you're probably seeing a lot of gay college ones :P

Jared   haha true to that just start zoneing out on the most fuckin retarded commercials.

Stacey   Hahahaahhahahyeaahh !Ahahaha that's probably what it is aha, but I think for the most part they're just the shittest actors ever ahaha!

Fritz   that's how half the movies out are like now a days though, shitty ass actors. I watch the movie baked and it's like, this is complete bullshit

Stacey   Ahahahahahahah that's like my life story ahaahah. I don't even know what to do high anymore, movies and tvsuck!

Fritz   that's why i avoid the TV it sucks. music is where it's at Stacey, music

Fritz   and food :D

Stacey   Bahaahah, illl remember that and ohhmygod food is amazing, Like If I could eat all day I would ahahahahah

Fritz   listen to some XV or talibkweli with a nice bowl of cereal. life is complete. food is my best friend. me too, that's what i plan on doing today, and stupid class work i'm missing :(just cooked up these potato and cheese filled shits on the stove with some oil, so fucking good.

Stacey   Hahaahahahahhahahaha! Cereal is gods gift to earth its like a drink and food all in one?!?! That sounds so bomb ahhahah I'm just sticking to hotpockets and waffles withnutellaaahahahaha.

Fritz   Ill check them out when I'm on my laptop ahahahaha

Mandy	Are yuuhiqhriqhtnow??
Stacey	are you high right now? Ahha
Mandy	Nopeee not yettlol.
Stacey	Ahahhahaha I love you Mandy♥
Mandy	Ily to stacey♥lol. Are yuuattskool?
Stacey	Ahahanaa, I go to a charter school waha
Mandy	Ohh lol. Im att home, jhuss chilln(: I hate skool lmao
Stacey	Ahahah me too , I just hated waking up eearly ahah
Fritz	throw some chocolate syrup into the cereal and it's perfect! chocolate milk and food in one thing. can't ask for more than that! you have no clue how bomb nutella and waffles sound, too bad the girls in this house eat nutella like it's nothing :(you don't go to THS anymore :O?
Mandy	Samee here, it qets so old, qotta like qet ready & shittuqhhh. Lol
Stacey	Ahhaahahahah, I seriously keep like 3 containers of nutella on deck at all times ahahahaah, That sounds so good! Chocolate milk with whip cream is supper amazing ahahah. And naaa :/ not until next year
Fritz	nutella on deck ahahahhaha just made me laugh. fuck can you handle a sack of nutella for me, don't skimp me. noooo hot chocolate with whip cream so it like melts into it making the perfect combination. what caused you to have to move schools?
Mandy	Lmfaowowwstacey! Ay its trueechocalate milk, w/ whip cream does sound qood lol.
Stacey	Bahahahaahah I wouldn't skimp you! I have threee whole containers ahahah, I'm a nutteellla dealer nbd. Ahhh I want one of those pizza cookies from bjsahahahahahaa And yeah it does huh Mandy!?!
Mandy	Bj'smhmmmm... Naajk. Lol hell yee it does("
Fritz	okay but i'm gonna bring my nutella scale, i've heard of you around the chocolate spread game. PAZOOKI, a party one with half oatmeal raisin quarter peanut butter, quarter chocolate chip. Mmmm

Stacey	Ahahahahahaha oh my gosh, I want one soobadd! Aahahah with ice creammm. Ahahahanooworriess I have some supper dankss!
Fritz	ughh this is making me hungry, time to make more food muahahaha :} getting off this network, text me if you'd like to! 555-5555
Stacey	bahahaohkay Fritz

Stacey	no wonder our town is filled with pothead, druggies, and alcoholics, there's nothing to fucking do! smh.
Mike	EXACTLY!!! HAHAH X)
Stacey	Ahhaah seriously its like the only exsiting thing to do for like 50 miless ahaha
Lauren	Haha Mike. Parking lot everyday(: Lol
Stacey	Ahha do you guys blaze in the parking lot ahaha
Mike	MOST OF THE TIME :PHAHA
Stacey	Well thanks for the invite :p
Lauren	Haha 99.9% of the time Lol and Stacey it's an open parking lot. It funny though because of that entire group I'm the only white girl haha
Mike	HAHA U WOULDNT BE DOWN!
Stacey	Ahhaha and why not!
Lauren	Some of the best time we have had have been in the parking lot Lol so much shit happens.
Mike	IDK HAHA IM JUST PLAYIN :P
Stacey	Ahahaohhohkaaay :) well I don't even go to your guys' gay ass school anymore ahaha
Lauren	Doesn't mean you can't come chill.
Daniel	Maybe if they built a fucking amusement park or something!
Stacey	OH MY GAWD,yes like a water park, lets bulid it Daniel, right after we steal my neighbors dog low key ahaha
Daniel	Yes! Deal:)
Daniel	it will be called... DANIEL AND STACEY'S NAKED PALOOZA!

Stacey	ahahahaha oh yeah thats so normal, get your ass over here and maybe we can construct it today ahaha1
Daniel	I neeeed a ride home! Hahaha
Stacey	ride my bike asshole haahaha
Daniel	Yeah fucking right!
Mike	HAHA OHH WAT SKOOL U GO TO?
Stacey	AHAAH a charter school, but its only three days a week so its striaghtaahah.
Bert	woah how doyou get into that school???
Mike	DAAMN SMARTY! :PHAHA
Stacey	bahahah thanks but anyone can get into it, you guys should switch into it ahahaha :)
Mike	TSSS! CHARTER SKOOL SOUNDS EXPENSIVE AND HARD X)
Stacey	Ahhaah its neither of those, its free its just liike a public school exsept its 3 days a week ahah

---

Jack	I love my best friend.Marjorie

Marjorie	I Love Youu Too Dear. We Gotta Fuck Shit Up Soon!
Jack	Let's do acid. and go on an adventure in the woods?
Marjorie	Okaii.

Stacey	I wannaa get high and eat ha.

Jonathan	eww
Stacey	No one asked you,
Jonathan	seems pretty gross... just sayin
Stacey	Fucking hipocritee, you hangout with tony, you definatlysmoke.
Zachary	That's sounds bomb ha
Stacey	Ahhaexsactly Zachary ahahahaha :)
Jonathan	ummm no I dont. its a waste of ur day it makes u sleepy, lazy and its really not that fun... ull understand when u get older xD

Stacey	Again, no one asked or wanted your opinion :) byeeeeee.
Zachary	It's enhances your life and opens ur mind to everything in a whole different way. And it makes food taste fuckin bomb. But Staceys right no one asked you
Jonathan	okay, dont try soo hard to be cool. ;) sooobyeee
Diether	I WANNA GET HEAD AND SLEEP
Diether	GIVE ME HEAD
Stacey	That'll be fiftyyy dollars. HA
Stacey	Fuckin love Zachary :) ahahaha
Diether	fuck that
Diether	give head like a champ
Stacey	Ahhaah fucking Diethers ridiculous. This is why you got hit by an orange. :)
Diether	lmao shut up(: datwasnt even me thoo
Stacey	Hahaaha yeah I kindaaguesssed with all your status's about fucking fatchicks, I meaan, I know you charge by the pound ahaha
Diether	ahahahayeahh me and this nigga had a lil facebookwar.
Stacey	Ahahha your cooool :) whyy were you guys doing that ahaha
Diether	cuhz we stupid lmao. So im guessing your not going tonight?
Stacey	Ahhahaahaha :) and no fml ahah, now I don't know whaat to do haha
Diether	fuck jus go(:
Diether	lmao
Stacey	Ahah that's whaat sierras trying to convince me to do aha, itd bloww if they made me leavee though aha
Diether	ohhh well, its not like you got anything to lose if you go. buhhdats all on you
Stacey	Ahahyeahh I knoww, I don't think I will though ahah, but now there not coming to my house party over summer ahha
Diether	aight then, what you gon do then? ha & ahahaha well dats what they get i guess
Bert	koolkids^
Stacey	BERT GTFO AND GO FUCK LINSEY AGAIN
Stacey	:)))))))
Bert	ewwww you heard about that??ohgodd....... nty:) dont want the clap

Stacey	ahhaah yeah everyone did... and bruh you already did it whats one more time aha..
Bert	it was one time too many the first time........ I learn from my mistakes unlike potheads^^^^^^^^^^^^^^^^^^^^^^^^
Stacey	hush up, id rather be a pot head then alot of other things SO THANK YOU. Byeahah
Bert	bye!
Stacey	:) !

Brittney	Just had a dream entirely about smuggling chicken eggs into Mexico....why...
Chase	chicken eggs full of heroin
Brittney	no...they were normal `chicken eggs...but when they cracked they looked like giant worms that looked like mandarin oranges...
Chase	I think someone has been doing too much heroin
Brittney	debateable
Owen	brittney was clearly on acid...
Rylie	xanniiezzzzzz
Tasha	HERRRRRRROOOOOOOOOIIIIIIIIINNNNNNN
Brittney	idont do anything but smoke weed though so...
Rylie	pawthead
Chase	well comon brittney all the cool kids do heroin
Tasha	i smoke br0wn all day
Arneth	U would:)haha
Jaypee	DISLIKE, DISLIKE, DISLIKE!!!!! Go to bed! I love you :)

Stacey	WEED IS BAD, don't smoke it. You will die. Just give it all to me. I'll suffer for you.
Daniel	Hahahadumbassss
Garret	lets shareee Stacey
Stacey	:)))))))))))))))))) you love me.
Rhanel	haah nice try but im keeping my delicious bud ;)

Charice	hahahha !cani suffer too
Daniel	NO, you didn't teextme
Stacey	damn aithhought this would ork, ahahi love you charice. and you didnt text me daniel
Brittney	Hahahahafuucckkyeesss
Daniel	I told you to teextme
Stacey	yessss britnneey yahah, SO DANIEL
Daniel	So text me asshole
Stacey	too much pride. wah. :O
Daniel	fine
Diether	you stupid lmao
Stacey	ahah you stupid Diether, im "healed" ahahhh
Diether	ahaha shut up, that was the proper word wasnt it?
Stacey	ahahah like if i went to get medicinal spices or something ahaha,
Diether	lmao shuttupp(: id say text me buh you never text back :b
Stacey	ahah okkaaay ill hush, but i was proving you just as stupid as meeahah :) and iwillll! my new phones just kicking my asssahah
Matthew	smoke fried eggs
Stacey	smoke weeeeeeed.
Matthew	I got hacked
Julia	HAHAHAHAHA i love this!!!!!!!!!!!!!!!!!!!!!!!!!!!!!!!!!!!!!!
Stacey	haahahah its the greatest :) but no ones given me theres yet :(
Julia	uh oh:(omglastnight i had a dream that all these people were giving me free weed!...and then i woke up and i had none;(i almost cried;(aha
Stacey	ahhahahaah that sounds horrrible! like sometimes that happens to me with fooodahahah. or phones. ill get like good ass food or a iphone, and i wake up with neither :(

Samantha	having sex with someone should always mean something, but most of the time it really doesn't and it's really fucking sad how low people are.

Arland	So truee, thats why its hard to find a truly honest girl in this town :/
Leo	*Anywhere
Samantha	that's why girls think it's okay to fuck basically anyone at any school.
Samantha	funny.
Colt	I hate bitches. It's suck for the nice guys out there.
Jairus	bitches be trippen
Jestone	I despise the way men act these days I appologize for the actions of mankind :/ I truly wish guys would be raised to be men with morals instead of boys who play around with peoples hearts and feelings...
Rowena	This makes me sad:(
Colt	Guys have to have appreciation for all girls before they can actually keep a relationship.
Samantha	Babyrowena I love you♥ and thank you Jestone you're my heroo
Rowena	Hes my hero too even though i dont know him.....i missed you today:((
Samantha	I think i was somewhat dying hahahah
Rowena	Why!
Samantha	I'll tell you tomorrow. I couldn't walk :)
Rowena	Ohh lordd! Okay<33
Jestone	Awww not even but thank you Samantha im truly sorry most guys are pigs these days and thank you also Rowena :) you two seem to be chill peeps ;)
Tony	im surprised no one's said this yet.....FUCK BITCHES GET MONEY!
Rowena	no tony. smh........
Samantha	Cute profile picture bff :)
Tony	shuttup rowena and thanks bff:)
Rowena	it loooks like your smellling her hair (;
Jestone	you just made yourself look really... unintelligent right now Tony was that really necessary?
Tony	i know rowena(; its cuz i have a hair fettish.and jestone,who the fuck are you? Ahhahah
Jestone	wouldnt you like to know lol

Tony	**no**
Jestone	**hahaha this makes me laugh**
Tony	**then we're on the same level! queer.**
Jestone	**didnt think so. Just saying why dont u try try something new and have some respect for women? You will earn more respect.**
Jestone	**Once again u sound like a jr. higher grow up...**
Rowena	**hehehehehe dis is funnny(; tony learn from dis kid♥**
Tony	**aight sounds good...ha**

Jack	**Never doing drugs, Smoking weed, Smoking cigs, Drinking anything. For a long long time.I could be in juvi right now.**

Jack	**I need to wake the fuck up. I've had too many warnings.**
Beatrice	**Story of my life. And I still don't learn.**

Brittney	**Mr. Doe from our Middle School got arrested for having sex with a minor whos a junior now too oh my god he was my teacher ewwewwewwwwwtffffffffffffff**
Kier	**hahahahahha FUCK DOE**
Eli	**hahahahahahaha damn!**
Ramon	**Did he fuck her when she went to that school or now?**
Reggie	**Must be disturbing recalling everytime he looked at you in class...lol**
Jenette	**Omg he was my faqvorite teacher!**
Brittney	**HES A FUCKING RAPIST I ALWAYS KNEW IT WOULD HAPPEN**
Brittney	**he's a rapist tho......awk.**
Ramon	**I wanna know wat age**
Ruby	**seriously brittney i have called this since i had him. i need to know who the girl is**
Ruby	**we have to know her or know of her.... like its not that big of a town.**
Brittney	**its been going on for a year meaning she was 16 when it started cuz shes 17 now and shes in my grade and he was both our teachers**

Ramon	Oh I thought he was having sex with her when he was her teacher

---

David	Wow just found out there's a registered sex offender that lives down my street. Time to Knuckle up!
Aubrey	ew
Brittney	tell him to hit me up...
Trey	theres a bunch in this Town
Ralph	get ur crazy neighbor that pulled a gun on me to shoot him
Philip	and you have a little sister!
Axel	Dude its trippy once you find out theirs Creepers in your neighborhood
Myla	People get registered as sex offenders for stupid reasons like if they pee in public....
David	Yeah I know and for real I'm gonna catch fades with this old white bastard
Ralph	really? ^ ha
Myla	No joke hahaha
Philip	haha
Axel	Hit me up when your about to get down so I can watch the fight
David	No this mofo is still Gunna get Molly whooped
David	Axel I live far from you
Axel	I don't give a fuck ill walk that shit no problem lol
David	Haha with 2 mickeys in your hands?!
Axel	2 mickeys in my hand one in each pocket and a grit on my lips lol
David	Eyyyhaha we gotta rage again like old times dog! It's been too long. Malt liquor=fun night
Eli	Do the sex offender shuffle!
David	I'll scrap him just like that one guy that one day! haha remember the sirens Eli?!
Eli	Haha that story made my day dude!!

Tony	Not trying to be corny but it actually is hotter everytime youre in my bed-I fuckin love Linsey!xD

BREAK UPS & MAKE UPS

Cole   I told you, I loved you, now thats all down the drain, ya put me through pain, I wanna let you know how I feel… Fuck what I said it dont mean shit now, fuck all the presents might as well throw em out, fuck all those kisses they didnt mean jack, fuck you you hoe I dont want you back.

Samantha   relationships end because once the person has you, they stop doing the things it took to get you.

Sherwin   Have had bad news but also really good news. Ya it sucks to get broken up with over Facebook but to know my stepdad doesn't have cancer makes everything better. Everything happens for a reason. Thankful!!

Cheryl   Flirtationship; More than a friendship, Less than a relationship.

Zane   ♥ Before Marriage ♥
Boy: At last i can Hardly wait!
Girl: Do you want me to leave?
Boy: No don"t even think about it!
Girl: Do you love me?
Boy: Of course, always!
Girl: Have you ever cheated on me?
Boy: No, why are you asking?
Girl: Will you kiss me?
Boy: Every chance I get
Girl: Will you slap me?
Boy: Hell no, are you crazy?!

Girl: Can I trust you?
Boy: Yes!
Girl: Darling!!
♥ After marriage Read It backwards!!

Samantha   if we loved again, I swear I'd love you right.

Sheena   For once I just want to be worth it. ♥

Samantha   I never left, you just stopped needing me.

Audrey   turning a friendship into love is a lot easier then turning love into a friendship.

Samantha   best way to not get your heart broken, is pretend you don't have one. bye fuck you.

Julius   u dnt seem lik a very happy individual! dnt be sad, be awesome
Samantha   nope i just hate everyone ahhaha.
Julius   true. it seems like everyone gives me a reason to hate em
Samantha   it seems like guys are pricks and girls are sluts
Julius   real talk mhm

Stacey   Relationships are like yard sales, from a distance they look great, but once you're in one, you realize its just a bunch of shit you don't need. Haaa

Joey   hahaha
Jess   smart thinkin right there
Stacey   Haahtoook a while to learn but I got it down now haha
James   damn hahahahXD

Samantha	you're leaving because it's easier to walk away, than to fight for what you really want.

Jomer	Then their a straight pussy!
Samantha	jomer, i love you more than salt crystals
Arnold	can i jack this post from you pleaseeeeee haha(:
Samantha	yes Arnold you're the homie♥
Arnold	nawww im good, i really like this post tho(:
Vhong	he leave cuz u nasty lol jk jk love u samantha! when are we guna kick it! Lol
Samantha	i do not know vhongg ahah♥

David	WOW, it's always cool to be cheated on... Nbd

Kendra	Really......
Jorge	God damn sluts
Mary	the worst feeling!
David	Yup all my friends tell me the same thing. Kinda hard to believe they all lied. Second chance=done
Rhea	dont call em sluts and whores for no reason
Rhea	hahaohh shittt
David	I'm not calling her a slut or whore. I'm just dissapointed and over being lied to
Jinky	you was wiff someone?
David	WAS
Andres	You need to choose your girls more wisely boo. Don't worry it will come to you one day. & if someone cheats on you then it's their loss not yours.
Lou	ew:/ forget that
Lou	txt me if you wanna talk love:/
Jinky	Lmao that's all bad , and the keyword within what Andres said is GIRLS , you need yourself a woman. Someone who knows how to hold their own as well as treat a man.
David	Okay♥
Jackson	jinky is super smart huh hahaha
David	Haha yeah she is

Leizel	:o
Leizel	honestly once a cheaater always a cheater, David you know you deserve the best and shes out there , you just got some obstacle courses to get through and will make you stronger and when you find her its going to be so worth it (:
David	♥ I sure hope (:
Leizel	I know so ♥
Kendra	shut up leizel
Leizel	funny thing is, this was your loss on him.
Kendra	thanks leizel <3
Jorge	Obviously you are a cheater too so why are you fighting it
Leizel	no problem, glad you realized it , AFTER you fucked up kbye♥ and uhhhgree Jorge (:
Kendra	bitch gtfo your just jealous
David	I honestly have never cheated... So get your facts straight Kendra.
Leizel	ahahahahha dude go away. your dumb, you fucked up, David deserves better and move the fuuuccckk on.
Kendra	this doesn't concern you, this is between me and David.
Leizel	and yeah it does concern me cause i care about him and his feelngs , unlike some people * COUGH COUGH *
David	Thanks Leizel ♥ I don't want everyone to fight I'm just over being disrespected by girls I date
Faith	Awe I hate that feeling you will find someone
Kendra	K bitch shut the fuck up... It wasn't your relationship so "go away"....♥
Jinky	@ Jackson, lol thanks ... I've been thru it all..
Leizel	no problem (: and no offense Kendra you look like the bitch here, im just lookin out for David (:
Jorge	She mad bro

Stacey	A relationship without trust is like a car without gas. You can stay in it as long as you want but it won't get you anywhere.
Clint	trueee im here if u need to talk Stacey like i told u like at 2 in the morning haha

Stacey	Ahahaha I know Clint your always there for me and I love you!
Clint	ilovee u tooo♥
Alvin	soo true ahaha
Bing	God damn Stacey fukn philosophical ass haha. Every1 listen 2 the wisdom of Stacey
Stacey	Ahahaahahawh thanks bing! Mwuaha ill always share my "wisdom" with you ahah
Mario	sounds about right
Stacey	It is Mario :)
Rylie	Wow.
Stacey	Oh hush.

Grace	What's up with your phone? And why is your ex posting immature bullshit on Facebook?
Jerran	phone will be turned on tomorrow. ill message you a temp. number
Cesar	Have you seen his ex? Lol she bitches about ppl creepin n then posts slut pics

---

Tony	that hillarious moment when your psycho ex girlfriend tries to fight your new way better girlfriend and gets her ass beat! HAHAHAHAH♥
Ram	FUCKING AWESOME/
Tony	especially since jane beat the shit out of me when she found out i cheated on her! she cheated first though so i'm not the bad guy;) Karma's a bitch! Ahhahahaha
Steve	cheating is still bad man, dont be too proud of it
Ram	Jealous Right!
Tony	i'm not proud of cheating! i'm proud of linsey for beating that bitch's ass!
Ram	wait wait woah woah when was this? i wanted to see it):

Steve	well violence doesnt solve anything, but if jane started it then its self defense, but ahh violence is dumb. peace and love and maturity is the way to get things done
Tony	yeah nigguh. PLUR LIFE♥ and yeah jane did start it
Steve	being that im not hip and i have no idea what that means
Tony	peace love unity respect. its a rolling term ahahhaha
Tony	but basically what you described. you'd make a perfect thizzheadsteve...seriously
Steve	hahahahaha yeah thats what everyone says. everyone already thinks im the biggest druggie anyways
Rolly	D:

Jane	Make up sex > closure sex.

Tony	is in a relationship withLinsey.

David	Dude no way haha
David	Props
Tony	Hahahahhahaha thanks shits been going really good:)
David	Ya dog I'm glad haha as long as she ain't with Brent. That kids a pussy fasho haha
Tony	Hahah I love you dude! I don't even know him but I kinda feel bad cuz she dumped him for me while I was basically with Jane still so I upgraded:D and she beat Janes ass earlier. I have the chillest girl ever;)♥
David	She did?! They actually fought? Hahaha
Linsey	yesss we did actually fight♥

Brittney	That awkward moment when your ex-boyfriend still thinks its acceptable to post on your moms wall...a year after you broke up. you've got to be fucking kidding me
Gerald	Thats always cool..

Brittney	like who the fuck does that........he like tries to be a part of my family.......but we hate him.....
Rylie	fuxxcckkkkkkhiiihhhmmmmuhhppp. hella.
Brittney	im like really fucking confused hes posted on her wall twice this week..
Gerald	Lol sounds like a good time
Randy	Let me put in the work
Brittney	what? Ahah
Randy	Like beat him up haha
Brittney	can you please do it
Gerald	@randy...lets take turns beatin that ass...lol
Jenelyn	hmmm lets guess who
Randy	Possibly but I need to break my hands in again
Brittney	"i miss eating all ur top ramen and making u buy me cheese that I didnt eat lol" is what he said. HONESTLY WHY DOESS HE NOT TAKE THE HINT THAT THATS NOT OKAY E7FG43BE8CWH7gryfbhrfvd
Gerald	Thats such a cute comment -___-
Brittney	like we literally broke up almost a year ago and we havent talked since...besides arguing......

Stacey	boys are stupid as fuck. if you like me, BE NICE. if you want to talk to me, TEXT ME FIRST. and if you want us to last, THEN DONT FUCK IT UP? not rocket science.
Fritz	but then girls make it seem like it's always an application, it's nice when the girl wants to also get to know the guy just as much and put in the effort. justsayin :D
Stacey	ahahai know maybe im being a bit general, not all guys, but the guys who have been around me lately ahah. sowwrrry Fritz :) and i know ahha
Katherine	couldn't have said it better
Stacey	love you a lot best friend♥
Fritz	ahh yes, no offense to them but most guys these days act... questionable. force girls to put up like 4 layer walls :/
Stacey	haha exactly Fritz :)! You gett it ahah!

Katherine	love you moreee (: "he's" really fucking weird i miss "him" and "he's" a straight up dick for not even remembering that...
Stacey	AHAHAHAH like we have so many problems with so many different people, its not even funny.
Swen	agree with Fritz.
Katherine	suckkkkyy darn darn. :(
Fritz	growing up with someone like Leesa lets you learn quick to avoid things that tick off girls, helps out in the end.
Stacey	ahahahahhaahhaahhah, your sister and leesa are so funny ahha!
Swen	true true, plus you have to put in that some guys just dont care and go crazy as well, when they should be patient
Stacey	ahahyeahh exactlyy.
Fritz	they're downstairs having a "jersey shore watching party" made me restart it half way through. i couldn't do it twice
Stacey	AHAHAHAHAHAH, thats so funny ahahahah. wwell if you see them again tell them i say hiiiahah
Fritz	probably will in like 5 minutes when munchies kick in and i want more girl scout cookies bahaha.
Swen	^^ thats where its at
Stacey	AHHAAHAHHA you are my favorite person ever, just sayin ahaha.
Swen	i almost bought like 20 boxes but they whre like 4 bucks
Jessica	can i marry your statuses.
Stacey	BAHAH only if i can marry yours girl!
Swen	Fritz make sure you get there befor there all gone
Jessica	HAHAH mine arn't even close to yours.
Stacey	yes theyre amazing!
Fritz	straight up they all charged in and snagged them. Sound of the boxes opening made me cringe.
Swen	i can feel your pain my sister stole and ate 3 of my boxes of carmel delights
Fritz	omg don't say the words carmel and delights in the same post. makes me wanna sprint and grab a box. only thing keeping me in this chair is eminem.
Stacey	ahahahaha well at least you guys have girl scout cookies in your house ahha, when my mom diets we all suffferrahhaah

Swen	^^ agian that where its at dude. For me its all bout the classic songs by him like cinderella man and 8 mile
Swen	and Stacey thatsprobally a good thing considering when they r in the house thats the only thing u wnat to eat and when there gone, your scrounded wanting more ahah
Fritz	Swen no no, anything off recovery doens't count as eminem
Swen	ahaha, or curtians up aswell
Daniel	Yooooooooou make it seem like its all the guys work
Stacey	well idk, relationships and shit are too much work. over it. going to sleep. Night everyone.
Daniel	Night:)
Bryan	....Forever..
Stacey	Aloneee?
Efren	Agreed Daniel. sounds hi maintenance

Donald	It's almost been one year since I lost the best girlfriend I've ever had, Thalia. These fucking dreams I keep having at night about it better stop cause I'm loosing a lot of sleep. I hate this time of year. Tough to say but I miss my cookie :)
Arland	Get better bro
Anastasia	:/ I sowwie. You'll spend forever with the one that's truly meant for you babe. You're young, you have plenty of time to find her ;)
Matilda	♥
Anastasia	Better be me though, just sayin. ;P jk :) love your face bess frenn ♥
Jolina	Don't you have a girlfriend?
Donald	No
Jolina	Well you Were like a week ago and it still says you are haha
Donald	Lol I'm just not in a rush to change it cause I'm to busy for a gf it pisses them off
Anastasia	^lol..
Donald	^fine example haha jk love ya Anastasia!
Skipper	Cookie cookie :)
Anastasia	bahahah..Love ya too bess frenn ♥

Lynette	Get over it already! ;) She was a nice girl but there is another one out there that is better!
Cassandra	What happened to Thalia? if you don't mind me asking..
Donald	I wasn't respectful towards her mom. So eventually her parents forced us to separate. Lesson learned tho
Cassandra	Omg. I thought she died. Hahaha don't be so dramatic damnit.
Donald	Hahahahah that would really suck! No but we don't talk at all. So after 4 years of dating that would bother u to :)
Cassandra	Haha no i'm only kidding. I totally understand. I just saw that post the other day and i was like wtf happened to her. I could've sworn she graduated hahaha,

---

Chester	Ive walked miles and miles multiple times to take buses and trains to see a girl who i thought cared...i baked a note in foil in a cupcake and took it all that way to ask you out in a cute way cause you have never been asked before in a cute way...after having a seizure and taking an ambulance ride to the hospital i still kept to my promise and asked you out to homecoming while you sat on my hospital bed....they didnt know what was wrong with me and i didnt care....i just was so nervous about asking you i didnt care about my health or why i was even there..even tho i couldnt afford it at the time i still found a way to take you..i left you the first time we dated because i had a drug problem and wanted to get clean before i dated you again cause i wanted to be better for you....you just found a new bf.....i still to this day have never kissed a girl since you....Id literally give an arm for you...Guess it just wasn't meant to be....i know everyone hates drama on facebook but ive gave up all my friends and just need to vent to something. ill shut up now. i love you Christina. Im sorry. bye.
Theodore	woooh my life with a girl with the same name... i got you man! :)
Chester	I remember that bro...lets skate again some day? hah
Mason	Bro!

Theodore	yeah i still have drama from that shit... but yeah i haven't skated in forever! but we will, i need to get a board and trucks first haha.
Nicholas	The funny thing is, she didnt read any of that. And if she did, the response was more along the lines of "lol ok"Srry man. We've all been there once.
Benjie	Chester, I think ur great. That takes some kahunas to do that man... I got mad respect for you... Ur very compassionate like me... I probably would have done the same for a girl I loved... I better see u at camp
Lorraine	:(I don't know Christina at all, I won't pretend like I do, but I'm almost positive that she must love you just as much as you love her. There's a reason why you guys made it this far, right? If you guys still love each other don't give up. Whatever this is, I'm sure it will pass and you guys will be back together soon. So, chin up!
Lemuel	you have a lot of people who love you bro...always remember that.
Lillian	Any girl would be lucky to have you. Keep your head up and remember that everything happens for a reason. If it's meant to be, it'll all work out. I admire you for having so much courage!
Bridgette	:(what's going on? Hope your ok.
Chester	Thanks everyone....ill be ok...i appreciate everything. Miss you Benjie ...
Benjie	I miss you man.. When I am 18 we need to get a tattoo together man
Chester	Im down...everyday i look at my tatts in my reflection i break down....but forsure we need to do that! that would be sick...
Queenie	holy shit! and just when i was beginning to think there were no good guys out there....
Chester	hah she doesn't think so...
Lemuel	You can do better....ive seen with my own two eyes how mean she is when you do nothing hah come on dude. you got this.
Queenie	boy, she trippin! but keep your head up man. N don't settle. Someone will come around that will appreciate everything you do for them(:

Bridgette	None of you know my sis or the situation......so shut it.
Lemuel	Chesters nothing but nice to her...shes just to young for him. Chester is one of the nicest people i know. With the kindest heart. I know him better then anyone.
Bridgette	I agree that he is a sweetie, but, I don't appreciate people talking about my sister. This is all about stuff that not everyone knows about so people need to be respectful with what they say.

Liam	I don't understand how couples can be so mean to each other when they break up...you say you cared about them last week now he's an asshole and she's a bitch? Idk why people can't break up on decent terms haha
Finley	i get it if something bad happened between them like cheating but other than that i think its dumb to hate eachother just cause u broke up.
Sandy	no one deserves to be treated like that.
Laura	Amen.
Andrea	ok Sandy
Liam	Ok Andrea :P haha
Freya	Hahahaha seriously. Miss you!
Peter	you can realize once you broke up that the other person is completely wrong and was far from a good boyfriend/girlfriend, but i think when you hate each other because you aren't together shows immaturity. so i just wanted to elaborate on your completely accurate post sir.
Liam	Miss you too Freya :) and Peter you got it bro! Haha
Sandy	okay Andrea.
Peter	dude next time you come back down how about you call me to hang out. i won't take up too much of your time
Liam	Hahaha Fa sho!
Alonzo	ME TOO BIG MAN!!
Rhea	i dont have hatred i care for them all and wish them all the best buttt i cant say they feel the same way ha
Malachi	It's because breaking up make you those things lol

Judith	When someones hurt or upset, the way they think becomes irrational.

Shella	i hate you leaving my house with so much negativity on your mind. i know my past is hard for you, and i know you think about it all the time. but it should be so obvious that i'm not that same person i was, and honestly you know that you've changed me into such a better person. i try so hard to make you realize that i would change anything about myself to make you happy...
Herbert	I really cant put into words how much this means to me^^^ and how absoutly happy this has made me if i ever hadf a doubt in my mind before its gone thanks to you i couldent be happier like literally smiling riught now :) and i love that you posted this on my wall theres nothing i like more than that. just hearing you say all these things makes me so happy to know i have you in my life and your not going anywhere ♥ it may not seem like it but i have trust issues to and its hard for me to forget and let go of the past but after hearing all this rigght now its really not in my mind anymore casue you have went above in beyond to make me feel waaaay better then i was when i left your house and i thank you for that babe.i said it once ill say it a million times i love everything about you i think your flawless your the only girl who gives me butterflies when i kiss her and the only girl i want to spend all my time with i love you from the bottom of my heart and your the only girl i can see my self being with and thats the honest truth ♥:)
Herbert	Oh and hands down that was the nicest thing ANY girl has ever said to me :)
Shella	you know i try my hardest to show you how i feel. and i know you felt terrible when you left my house so i just wanted to show you that i care and i'll always try my best to make you happy even when your upset about me. ♥
Herbert	i really truley honestlky couldent ask for anything more :) like i said your pefect and im falling head over heels for you ♥
Shella	you're more perfect ♥ and i'm falling just as hard.

Herbert	dont worry baby ill be there to catch you i wont let you fall ♥
Shella	♥ thank you. i trust you.
Herbert	good i would do anything to keep your trust and to keep you :)
Shella	you have me ♥.
Herbert	you have me to ♥
Howard	You two are disgustingly precious. You make me throw up rainbows if that makes sense. Herbert, hold on to her buddy. :)
Shella	aww. ahahaha. I'm hoping that's a compliment! thankkkyou
Howard	Its a huge one, and youre welcome. Just take care of my boy there, he's like a little brother to me., and i know he just wants a girl to love and make happy. So smile, cause he chose you. ;p
Shella	considering to clasdify myself as the luckiest girl alive to be able to be in his life. I'm doing my best to make him happy:)
Howard	Im sure if the reasons youre smiling are cause of him then he'll be just fine. :)
Herbert	trust me im fine shes the best thing that ever happened to me truely :) and would do anything to keep her

---

Salvador	So fed up with everything. What do I do wrong?
Rudy	It ain't you bud. You already know that. ;)
Amor	I couldn't possibly know ANY LESS about your situation however I was once, many MANY Years ago a psycho girlfriend!!! LOL Try not to own more than your share of the issues sweetie!!! I promise you this will pass and you will look back and laugh at how little you have ACTUALLY done wrong!!
Maricar	You need to let go of the one that's complaining we know who SHE is !
Maricar	You are just starting your journey and having fun! Life is to precious and also has so much to offer and you don't need someone to bring you down ! You deserve BETTER! Dad and I Love U
Zander	Mmmmmmm.....SWAG!
Linsey	/: oh. Well yeah Salvador, I was mad last night. At Tate tho. I wanted to hangout with you and Tate messed that up for us.

But I didn't really do anything wrong except for be upset about an unchangeable situation.Maricar & Nate, I wanted more than anything for you guys to like me. But honestly you have every reason to hate me. I'm really sorry for everything that has happened. But I'll leave all of you guys alone now becoz obviously I'm never gonna fit in with your family. I tried my hardest to make a good impression but it wasn't good enough so I'm sorry. I understand that it isn't easy seeing your kid grow up becoz of what I've put my dad thru.

Linsey   But honestly last night I heard what you said about me Maricar. I heard you call me a slut and say that you fucking hated me and that you wanted me and Salvador to break up becoz "who knows how many guys have been in me." And you know what, that hurt REALLY badly. Especially to hear my boyfriends mom say that. And behind my back too. I think it was really messed up of you to say that but I know you have reasons for it so I don't even mind. I respect you both a lot as parents becoz you always do what's best for Salvador and you seriously have raised an AMAZING boy. He's so polite and so perfect. And I wish I could prove to both of you that I'm not as evil as you think I am...maybe if you would have given me a litttle more of a chance and actually talked to me more you could see that. I understand that you want me and Salvador to break up...I really don't want to /: but you know what's best for him more than I do, so I guess I'll let you guys make that decision /:

Linsey   I just want you to know that you're taking away the best thing that's ever happened to me tho. But I understand why. He probably wants to leave me anyways. I just want all of you to know that I'm really sorry for everything.

Salvador   We could talk, she rather fuss.

Salvador   I'm obviously the worst boyfriend in the world isn't that apparent?

Linsey   an amazing boyfriend. an understanding dad, and some hot chocolate ♥ my life is fucking awesome.

Linsey   what a slap in the face. </3

Miles   Txt me boo

Linsey	Okay /:
Linsey	I wish I could go back in time and make everything better :(
Jane	hey. I fucking love you ♥ you know I always got your back in situations..so you should text me & tell me what's been going on. I would have but my phones been acting stupid.
Linsey	I love you a lot and I will text you right now baby ♥
Linsey	yay my life is pretty much over. the best and only good thing i had in my life is being taken away from me. someone text me /:
Stacey	text me?
Miles	Love you♥
Linsey	love you lots Miles ♥

Audrey	babygirl, i know you feel like your life is ending but i promise you that everything will get better and you will be okay eventually. it may seem hard to believe but everything in life happens for a reason, even if it feels like its the worst thing in the entire world. when one door closes another one opens. i understand completely what you're going through, trust me so if you ever need anyone to talk to, ill listen. i love you so much, you deserve the best and everything will be okay. i promise ♥
Linsey	Thank you so much Audrey ♥ You are so sweet, it makes my day like a million times better to know I have amazing friends like you ♥ I love you a lot and I'm gonna text you after I shower :) Miss you baby :(thanks for being there for me. ♥
Audrey	you're welcome, i just want you to know that you really do deserve the best and i love and miss you too. we're hanging out next weekend, ♥
Linsey	yessss please ♥
Lauren	Hey girl, text me if you need anyone to talk to♥ my life is pretty horrible right now too so I know what you're going through and I feel bad because nobody deserve to be in this much pain ever, so I'm here for you(:
Linsey	Thanks Lauren ♥ I'll text you right nooowww ♥

Gwen	I love you so much babydoll♥ I would say text me but I don't have my texting so call me if you ever want to talk. I'll always be here for you<3333
Linsey	Thanks love♥ I'm gonna call you right now coz I miss you):
Gwen	Okay baby♥
Linsey	I really need to stop taking the things I have for granted.
Linsey	best night in a while♥ boyfraaann left a while ago and now movies with my witttle brother.

Linsey	Damn, going thru looking at my fb posts in the past 24 hours, I am one bipolar bitch. ahahah anyways, best friend is coming over now and boy friend is coming over laterr♥ yay :)

Linsey	baby tonight was perfect :) !then again, any time we're together is always amazing. I'm so happy you don't let other people get to you and that you're still with me after everything. I pwomise I'll be a better girlfriend. and I think I kindaaaa showed you that toniight. I'll keep proving it to you tho coz I love being with you. and I really don't wanna lose you. you're the best babe :) text me when you get home to let me know you're safe! ♥ xoxo muahh

---

Samantha	i want to kiss you on December 31st from 11:59pm to 12:01am, so i can have a great ending to 2011 and an amazing beginning to 2012♥

Brittney	If you dump someone over a text message or a phone call or a Facebook message you're a fucking pussy....if you can type it you can say it out loud. Pathetic!
Virgil	You tell em!!!
Brittney	I always do!!
Davion	AMEN SISTA AMEN!

Fabian	Brittney.... we need to talk....
Brittney	IS THERE ANOTHER GIRL? HUH? IS THERE?
Brittney	Sick
Richard	ironic
Fabian	no... its another guy :/
Drexler	It's over.
Brittney	How is it ironic Richard?
Larry	lol hey try saying 3/4 of ur statuses to your parents and see what happens. live by your own rules
Richard	that happened to me haha
Brittney	What are you talking about Larry?....and who are you...
Larry	im pretty sure in your pictures you have two eyes.... which means unless your illiterate you can read soo scroll up the page and read it once over
Richard	Andrea
Larry	and you said if you can type it you can say it out loud so how about going to your parents and saying hey wanna roll a blunt and see what they say
Richard	Larry you should probably stop ahaha
Drexler	Lololololol
Brittney	Who the fuck are you ha. Ya if I can type it I can say it out loud and anything I post on Facebook I do say out loud so you can fuck off and stop being a dick considering I don't know who the fuck you are
Andrea	Larry youre fucking annoying like seriously get off facebook or stop commenting on everyone's shit
Larry	lol so you add people on facebook who you have no idea who they are just so you can get attention in your litty pissy fit statuses you post 15 times a day. thats cute and you wonder why you get the shitty guys you do
Jovanni	Dtf......anyone?
Richard	lol
Brittney	If you're gonna be a dick then why the fuck did you send me a friend requests you fat redneck piece of shit...oh my god
Andrew	Titties. They make the world go around, god kid go look at some.

Andrea	delete her if you don't like it. im pretty sure adding people on facebook is a twoooo way street soooooo....? &you don't even know her shut the fuck upppppppppp
Richard	StartingFacebook Fights
Brittney	I've never even seen his name before anywhere to be honest so liiiiiiike...
Jovanni	He was trying to see tits isnt that why we all added Brittney?
Andrew	Im telling you, once he sees titties he'll simmer down.
Brittney	Bye Jovanni
Richard	i had english with larry last year and he had to sit in the corner away from everyone
Brittney	I don't understand what his fucking problem is?...
Andrew	He has a small dick, therefore he tends to be a rather large one.
Brittney	Good hypothesis
Andrew	My calculations seem to be correct...
Larry	that maybe true tests havnt come back yet
Andrew	Havnt
Larry	oh hey Brittney which dude was last night did u get his name first
Brittney	What the fuck?
Andrew	Hah what a damn tool, you don't gain coolness by being a prick to people...
Larry	so Brittney are you always with douche guys just wondering
Brittney	Fuck off.
Larry	you get what you deserve and if your a bitch you get douche bag guys but i can tell math isnt your thing
Brittney	I'm not a fucking bitch but I'm not gonna be nice to some guy who I don't even know that's a total dick to me when I've done literally nothing to them. You're fucking pathetic.
Andrew	Tooltooltooltooltooltooltooltool
Morris	brocclii and cheese
Larry	so your not a bitch yet you post statues like this every day and you wonder why you dont get good guys. oih and hey http://www.grammarbook.com/english_rules.asplearn some proper english Expand Preview
Roy	Haha happened to me too Roy. Twinning?
Andrew	As you spell oh "oih"

Brittney	What the fuck is your problem....
Larry	im the guy who shows you that your a bitch and you hate me but later in your life when your with a douche bag guy and you hate your life your gonna wish that you listened to me and even took your own advise
Morris	dude your penis is very tiny thats why your angry just go away
Andrew	You're* x2, advice*
Morris	leave Brittney alone ;) unless you think im a bitch who gets dousche bag guys too ;)
Larry	Morris good spirit Brittney might go for you now if she already hasn't she probably cant remember
Morris	Brittneys my siter
Morris	*sister
Morris	now you must pay
Brittney	That shows me I'm a bitch? I've done nothing fucking wrong to you...I'm not "with" anyone so I don't know what "douche bag guy" you're referring to, but I guess since I'm such a bitch I deserve to be alone right? Stop worrying about me and work on fixing your own problem first. You're pathetic. Bye.
Morris	bambambam
Andrew	My god you are a literal prick, way to attempt to criticize somebody on their grammar; then proceed to have multiple grammatical errors.
Larry	man and she calls me the redneck lolol
Morris	arent you larry the cable guys son?
Jovanni	Brittney hates mexicans. and gooks. fuck you all
Andrew	I'd be a bitter person if i couldn't see my own weiner while showering too.
Morris	wouldnt we all
Larry	hey Morris i noticed your parents are split up because Brittney and you have different last names does that affect your love life with your sister
Larry	Andrew is my favorite person in this because she is obviously putting me in my place with these well thought out comments
Brittney	Why are you still commenting on my status
Morris	i wish i could eat you alive.
Andrew	She...

Larry	lol ur a dude man your profile pictues say other wise
Larry	Morris im sure you wish you could maybe next time champ
Brittney	Go away
Morris	hahahah champs my middle name.
Morris	nobody calls me that.
Morris	i no im done now sorry Brittney i was bored and saw virgins trying to fight you so i thought id partake
Andrew	Yea you jackass i'm a guy, clearly im wearing a damn hat and kissing my son. As in your profile picture you're laying on what your $4.99 clearance inflatable raft from K-Mart? Twat.
Larry	vigin>loose af she would probably know
Brittney	I DON'T FUCKING KNOW YOU
Andrew	Brittneys tighter than your clogged arteries, fatass.
Morris	the end...
Larry	Andrew that thing is called a white water wrating boat. these is this thing called google it helps a ton
Larry	oh and hey Andrew is your son with Brittney or was it just a weekly fling not 100% sure
Cameron	why don't you just block this douche...
Andrew	White water rafting, and what was that, your ridiculous grammatical error confused me? These is this thing called google...what. Titties.
Brittney	I'm on my phone and on the phone and it keeps freezing when i click his profile and I broke my computer :(
Larry	http://lmgtfy.com/?q=white+water+raftingExpand Preview
Andrew	Say one thing about my son and i promise you that i will find you.
Brittney	Youre fucking disgusting
Larry	and hey you dont have to be an e-thug its not my fault you got your girlfriend preggo at 16
Brittney	What the fuck is your fucking problem wtf burn in hell
Larry	hey Brittney this was fun and i hope you learned something
Andrew	Didn't say it was bud, and she was 17, honestly you should think real hard about the next comment you send.
Larry	i will do the job for you and block you i wont block your e-thug buddies because they make me giggle

Cameron	Larry, honestly you should just stop. you've said enough. i don't know exactly what point your trying to make, but i can assure you, you sound like a complete ass hole and things you are saying aren't a joke, your harrassing.
Brittney	Fuck yourself
Jovanni	That was the most fucked up thing ive seen on facebook
Andrew	Not me, someone sent me a blue waffle through facebook..
Jovanni	Oh thats pretty fucked up ahahahahah
Brittney	Aaaaaand he blocked me
Cameron	good! that was so rude.
Brittney	I literally have no idea who he is
Cameron	he's bored with his life

Donald	You know, I've only said "I love you" to a few girls... Those words are strong and you guys use them way to easy. It takes time. And if your not with that person anymore, and you don't miss them, or think of them here and there- you never meant it...
Chuck	true that
Lucille	awh that so sweet made me smile. Told you, you are a great person and have an amazing heart
Donald	Yeah somewhere in there lol. It only comes out for ppl that deserve it ;)
Lucille	Haha yeah I guess people just need to stick around even when you do try to push everyone away.
Donald	I don't necessarily push people away, i talk to anyone that says hi.. But I limit the people I get close to and ppl I trust, it's a big difference :)
Lucille	When your mad or stressed you push people away. Well you don't like to talk about your feels and I push your buttons but still haha you know I'm always here for you(:I hope you know your one of the few people I trust bc of everything we've been through(:
Nanette	Not really cuz i loved my ex and was faithful for 2 years to get screwed over and lied to and cheated on i fell out of love as hard as i fell in.

Donald	Sorry to hear that must of been an idiot cause your very cute!
Nanette	He is an idiot!!!hahaha
Nanette	& thank u u too :]
Alondra	HA!
Donald	*Excluding shari :) lol
Jess	ohhhh i see stealing my lines !ahahaha

You may not be her first, her last, or her only. She loved before she may love again. But if she loves you now, what else matters? She's not perfect - you aren't either, and the two of you may never be perfect together but if she can make you laugh, cause you to think twice, and admit to being human and making mistakes, hold onto her and give her the most you can. She may not be thinking about youevery second of the day, but she will give you a part of her that she knows you can break - her heart. So don't hurt her, don't change her, don't analyze and don't expect more than she can give. Smile when she makes you happy, let her know when she makes you mad, and miss her when she's not there." - bob marley.

"I believe that everything happens for a reason. People change so that you can learn to let go, things go wrong so that you appreciate them when they're right, you believe lies so you eventually learn to trust no one but yourself, and sometimes good things fall apart so better things can fall together."
-Marilyn Monroe

Becky	it's better to be slapped by the truth then kissed with a lie

---

Parker	If someone understands your bullcrap, sticks around through all your mistakes, and smiles even though you've done nothing for them, than it's obvious they're a keeper. But it's also obvious that you don't deserve them.

Rylie	Ex boyfriend's and girlfriends never have anything nice to say anymore. Like 10% actually are still nice. the 90% just turn to worst nightmares.

Julia	AMEN
Dillon	please tell me im not on the nightmare side ;)
Rylie	lolwut?
Dillon	oh... you know ;)
Dexter	or that 1% don't even talk about it. Like me
Stacey	"hey ex boyfriend" " fuck you bitch"
Paolo	yeah get like me and dexter!

LOL

Drake	I want to make a facebook profile under the name of "nobody" so when people post pointless shit, I can like it and it will say "nobody likes this"

Vaughn	No matter how much i turn off my computer, And get bored of Facebook-I end up on Facebook like 5 minutes later.
Wendell	same haha
Maxxwell	Facebook brainwashes you into thinking you have a notification and you must see it ...

Drake	If lesbians arent attracted to men, why are they attracted to women that look like men?
Assunta	Thats what ive always wondered...
Dana	cause they still have vaginas
Korina	chuz they want a man with a vagina:)
Drake	Not like you can pork a vagina with another vagina
Edison	Scissor...
Patricia	hahahhaah
Leizel	just like when straight girls are attracted to girly looking guys, they still have a penis . and lesbiens dont think guys are ugly , they just arent attracted to penis's , just like gay guys think girls are pretty doesnt mean they wanna bone them. your not attracted to what they look like . yes you might think a girl likes another girl cause they look like a girl , no it doesnt matter what they look like . its just what your sexually attracted to
Darius	ohmygod you got so many likes over something so weird hahaha

Jedney	**Cause you have a vagina! Ewww**

Drake	**You were so beautiful until your 30 day trial of Photoshop ended.**

Brittney	**When a girl says "what?" it's not because she didn't hear you, she's giving you one chance to change what you just said....lolz**

Drake	**8 hrs until MW3 = the loneliness of the female population**

Drake	**When teachers say "I'm only giving you an hour of homework tonight", bitch do you realize we have 7 other people pulling the same shit**

Drake	**Fuck "ILY" and "IMY" if you really love or miss me, you would have spelled that shit out.**

Carmen	**God created man, and then said "I can do better than that" and created woman.**

Christa	**hhahahaa love ♥**
Carmen	**girls rule, boys drool(;**
Willard	**ouch.**
Eli	**u mad**
Reggie	**he was obviously referring to women's kitchen skills.**
Bert	**haah then women became sluts and God looked down and went SMH**
Carlo	**then created you and said i can def do better then that...**
Carmen	**lawlz. dueces.**
Deacon	**is that why Eve partook of the forbidden fruit? a greater problem?**
Eli	**This is the truest status that I have ever read**

Carmen	Carlo just because you think your the shit because you hangout with the "cool" kids doesnt mean you have to be a douche like all your other friends(:
Dainton	Haha he only made you to Provide for us sexually and make us food why do you think eve was getting the apples
Dale	Hahahahah ^^^
Eli	He made females so we can punch them in the stomach at lunch
Laura	Hahaha Carlo, hater.
Eli	#likeabitch
Carlo	hah what??
Carlo	def not a hater
Kirk	then he created me..
Colleen	Oh my gosh Eli hahahahahahahahahaa
Mason	Well cause he knew when he created the man he knew they were gonna be hard workers and need food to be cooked and sex to be ready so he gave us a female. Ahahaha jk jk
Laura	You're comment was a little too real... Hahah
Carlo	ha what do you mean?
Scarlett	i loveEliso much♥ hes the greatest boy in the whole wide world♥
Colleen	Hi Scarlett.
Sandy	CLEARLY YOU HAVE NEVER MET A BLACK WOMAN, jk love you Carmen and everyone else on this status even if i don't know you.
Colleen	I love you too Sandy.
Shelly	lol at Eli. hahahahahahahahhaha
Lysander	YES brookie ;)
Junie	you got your story wrong there...
Dawson	Lmao

Drake	Almost 18, definitely donating sperm to pay for my new car.
Dennis	wait, so what does giving sperm have to do with getting money?:D
Drake	A lot of bitches would pay for my genes!

Gretchen	ahahahaha
Gina	you are officially the weirdest kid I've ever met .
Bryson	best damn idea ever
Bentley	you have to be a certain height, and depending on the pharmacy, they have differnt physical traits that they look for, along with diseases that run in the family etc..ive looked into it -.-
Terence	good idea
Hank	Hope they don't have a time limit on how long it takes you, you might have pay them.
Benjamin	Haha you have to have a college degree I think. If not.. Lets go together.. Dutch Rutter?

Drake	That moment your in the gym and the girl next to you starts moaning like a t-Rex in heat

---

John	Women always say that giving birth is way more painful than a guy getting kicked in the balls. Here is proof that they are wrong. A year or so after giving birth a woman will often say, "It might be nice to have another child." You never hear a guy say, "It might be nice to have another kick in the nuts."

Drake	I like how girls get brand new 2012 models cars when they get their license and 80% of them are totaled by the end of the year

---

Drake	Some girls really do need make up

Crispin	some need make up inside
Tope	some just shouldnt even exist
Gina	some guys do too.
Baron	HAHAHAHAHAHAHA.
Gloria	Hahahahaahahahahahahahahahahahaaha
Crispin	hey not cool! jkjk yep goes both ways

Baron	this probly ruined someones day/self esteem,
Hilda	Hahahaha I love this status.
Drake	Crispin that's what men are here for
Crispin	amen^^
Andy	Oh Drake

Elmer	Boy: Lets play the firetruck game
	Girl: How do you play?
	Boy: I run my fingers up your leg and you say redlight when you want me to stop...
	Girl: Ok :)
	Few seconds REDLIGHT!
	Boy: Firetrucks don't stop for redlights ;)

Stacey	i now believe you when you say you love me because you just texted me back while you were playing xbox. ahahahha.

Drake	It must be so hard being 15 and not being able to find the love of your life...
Andrew	Even harder when youre a dumb bitch....or fat
Andrew	85 likes in 15 minutes...sex me
Drake	Id rather lick you
Madelyn	hahahah
Dewey	hahahahahahahahah
Dewey	This deserves all 204 of its likes.
Simeon	Even harder when ur a whore too
Marimar	AMEN
Ricky	I refuse to like this just because of how many people already have and i dont want the notifications but its a likeable post my friend ha
Drake	I'll like your comment to make up for it ♥. I saw your truck at school friday and I creamed my panties
Ricky	Isnt is it amazing ?!?!(!? :D

Drake	Yeah fucker. I need a decent vehicle haha
Ricky	Bro i was so stoked. Dude my truck was the most stock and unnoticable truck out there but a little time and money and a birthday ha and look at it now. Get on it homski
Benedict	242? The fuuuck i wish i had 2000 friends to like my shnazz
Drake	I would be too shithead, you got a newish tacoma with sick tires, nice interior, and a system. I would be pretty pumped too
Darius	why did so many people like this...
Ricky	I put so much money into it tho bro hah like dammmm....

Tony	I was just talking about Eli's milf and she was right behind me but I didn't know it...how fuckin awkward!
Daniel	Is She that hot?
Chloe	yes she is
Mitch	forsure^^^

Mariel	halloween is every girls excuse to dress like the slutts they really are (;
Evelyn	Ahahha not every girl:)
Mariel	mmhmmmm, suuureee.
Evelyn	Ahahahaa it's true
Marsha	Its the only time of the year we can go in our "birthday suits" and not get judged hahaha

---

Rebecca	I'm being a bitch for halloween. No costume ;)
Rylie	damn, you out did yourself on that one... ♥
Rebecca	Oh I know♥

Drake	Is tonight just "take a million years to reply" night or what.

Stacey	**Going to mcdonalds for a salad is like going to a hooker for a hug. Mwuahaha**

Melanie	**you should cover yourself in baby powder and be cocaine for halloween♥**
Jack	**Can I wear pasties over my nipples?**
Melanie	**yes<33**

Belinda	**SEXY AND I KNOW IT**

David	**Whose awake? Talk to me yeah?(: Idc of I don't know you let's change that**

Carlton	**In That Daily Game Chess Still Checkin For A Mate.**
Omar	**Searching for that queen.**

Landon	**I think im just gonna message some random old person calling them a bitch**
Kaleb	**YES**
Landon	**i already picked out a lady from oceanside... her life will be a living hell muahahahaha**
Kaleb	**you're gunna give her a heart attack**
Landon	**hopefully she has life alert!**
Tanner	**Your so cool Landon**
Landon	**i love you**

Rosie	**The more boys I meet, the more I love my dog.♥**

Lily	**MY DOG**
Lauren	**Lol♥**
Rosie	**The more I love Lily's Dog.**
Lily	**that's better. (:**
Rosie	**I need something of yours that is mine now.**
Lily	**at least buy me dinner first haha**
Rosie	**Take me out to dinner and maybe i will.**
Derek	**keep it that way :)**
Lily	**stop cheating on me with $leepy and maybe i will.**
Rosie	**Maybe if you actually asked me, I would have told sleepy I was already taken.**
Rosie	**:D.**

Linsey	**lalala I hate english. someone bring me food and a pillow**

Parker	**Someone just asked me if im going trick or treating tomorrow..... Fuck ya im going trick or treating!**

Brad	**that awkward moment when you get in the van and there is no candy**

Audrey	**if your boyfriend wants you for your breasts legs and thighs send him to kfc. you're a lady, not a cheap value meal.**

Brittney	**Watch nobody from my school ask me to Homecoming... just watch.**
Kyle	**i asked 45 girls last year and I was on the court and almost won homecoming king lol they all said no.**
Melissa	**i was just talking bout how no one is gonna ask me.................**
Drew	**I soooooo will**
Bam	**Kyle isn't lying ^^^**

Brittney	seriously kyle? or are you kidding, hahaha Melissa i already know noone will drew no offense but idont know youuu....
Brittney	bam omg
Louie	Winter formal's all that matters.
Drew	I know iwas jk
Brittney	winter formals not for a while
Kyle	I am being perfectly honest...
Brittney	:o kyle if you aske3d me iwouldve gone with ya cuz your cool n stuff
Hayden	I would ask you but due to your popularity and my shitty life. It would just make my life a whole lot shittier. just putting that out there.
Kyle	well now I've graduated and i can't ask anybody! so they just have to come ask me because I am a tool and I would gladly go with ANYBODY.

Jerran	i need the cock so bad right now
Tyler	don't yall love hackers
Karey	hahai knew it
Blake	haahhaahhahhahahahahahhahahahahaha

Stephan	"Thats the thing with women there tough to live with and tough to live with out" Grandpa knows what's up :]

Trisha	I wish there was an "easy" button to turn ur feelings on or off..

Tony	Thanks to whoever wrote "choke on it fucker" with a huge dick on my car♥
Steve	im sure its barely noticable! hahah
Darius	wtf....

Tony	**Nah it was in huge pink writing and my mom decided to clean it off cuz it was obscene and she got really pissed at me:)**

Colleen	**Waking up to your screaming kitten who fell in the toilet.... LOL HAPPY HALLOWEENZ**
Jordyn	**Crap she fell in the toliet(no pun intended) she is on my bed :(**
Colleen	**She has poopy pauwwz (;**

Brittney	**Some baby at McDonalds has been staring at me for five fucking minutes.......**
Bryan	**Little kids have no fucking shame.**
Eli	**Relax it's a fucking baby Brittney haha**
Steve	**cause you know, watching someone eat food, isnt creepy anymore at all**
Brittney	**Its not even fucking blinking guys....**
Andy	**stare back at it and see who blinks first**
Jacob	**babies sense fear**
Alwyn	**KILL THAT FUCKER**
Mitch	**babies hate sluts....**
Brittney	**K bye mitch.**
Eric	**Dont make any sudden movements**
Patrick	**hhaha look at all these corny ass lines ahahaha**
Eric	**Patrick.**
Brittney	**You guys all suck**
Patrick	**Eric**
Eric	**Sup**
Patrick	**text me lol**
Eric	**Hahaaight**
Tristen	**You're at McDonalds... thats your first problem.**
Brittney	**-____- I like McDonalds**

Samantha	**boys in beanies > boys in snapbacks.**

Andrei	beanies are the ish.
Samantha	they make me wanna love everyone
Andrei	haha. ide choose a beanie over any snapback. they are so much fresherrrrr
Samantha	snap backs are stupid
Andrei	i like snap backs dont get me wrong but i like beanies more. they look better. alot people cant rock beanies tho. haha. they rock em like they are 40 and they look like cone heads ahaha
Samantha	but only faggots wear snapbacks beanies make guys automatically 80 times hotter unless you have a really cute face then you can wear snapbacks.
Logan	Beanies and snapbacks !
Andrei	well im ugly soooo yeah i rock da beanies haha.
Samantha	no boys who wear snapbacks and kissable just once, but if you wear beanies then you want spend the whole night withh..
Samantha	don't put yourself down silly♥
Trey	I wear snapbacks wife:(
Samantha	but you have a cute face...♥
Trey	Oh well then it's okay cause I love beanies too!
Samantha	ahahah otay♥
Nicole	Depends on the boy
Samantha	exactly! but i perfer beanies♥
Nicole	I want a snap back for me :3 & ilove beanies & fitteds
Marco	im wearing a beanie right now:) hahah
Fritz	cause everyone wears basketball and hockey snapbacks, thus making them silly.
Samantha	hahahah fritz why do i love you♥ and yay♥
Fritz	because we are lovely people ♥ this man on the moon snapback is so sexy
Dick	Wow :'(
Samantha	YOU HAVE A CUTE FACE AND YOU KNOW YOU DO
Donnel	But I love my Versus snapbacks.......
Samantha	but i love you and you're adorable so its okay donnel♥
Donnel	♥ love you Samanthaaa
Donnel	I just read your previous comments. You broke my heart </3 haha
Andrei	I'm just ugly so it's all good

Donnel	^^^ Samantha just likes to put us down bro, don't worry about it. Your sexy and my Versus snapbacks are the shit bahaha
Andrei	I don't even know savanna haha. But she seems cool butttttt she doesn't like snapbacks soo that may become a problem.
Darius	alot of good looking girls liked this status so i'm going to wear my beanie more... cause im not attractive enough for a snap!:)
Samantha	hahaha i like you better in a beanie but you still look good in a snapbackckk
Darius	tanks:) i actually ordered a beanie 2 days ago so im good♥

Brittney	Only I would ask some random kid I don't even know if the huge thing on his neck was a hickey....his answer was "I went paintballing." YEAH OKAY RANDOM SLUTBOY
Nicole	hey asshole -____- this exact situation = me .
Chad	He probably was telling the truth haha
Jonas	Hahahaha! Hey brittney wana go "paintballing" ??? ;)
Brittney	Uh I've been shot in the neck with a paintball and I also have a hickey you can tell the difference. No Jonas....no
Nicole	I got shot in the neck and it looked like a fucked up hickie, it was just darker by a bit
Brittney	cool
Nicole	ha yea. verry>:)
Charlie	Ha, paintball leaves a pretty perfect circle.. Not an aboeba shaped thing hahahah..
Brittney	EXCACTLY

Jane	When you call your ex bf for help... that's when you know it's bad. Omfg.

Samantha	i love when boys smell really fucking good♥
Rowena	paris hilton = sex
Samantha	i seriously think of fucking somebody when i smell it.........

Rowena	i feeeel exactly the same...tell dewit to bring it tommoro!!
Samantha	dewit ahhahahah faggot
Rowena	hahahahaha oopssies(;
Samantha	i giggled
Rowena	teheh.....cunt♥
Susanne	me too...
Samantha	you too waht>
Susanne	I love when boys smell really fucking good
Colt	I use the cologne called "very sexy for him" it's smells pretty damn sexy.
Samantha	we have a lot in common susanne and FUCK you must smell very sexy
Colt	I must admit, I always do.
Chris	cologne has always been my thing since i was in like 4th grade haha, but my best smelling is gucci,i have to always smell good like 100% of the time.
Samantha	nope nope nope its fucking paris Hilton
Chris	paris hilton makes a guys cologne? if so and you think it smells good ill buy it haha
Samantha	it seriously smells like gods vagina
Chris	so im guessing thats a yes to them making a guys cologne haha? whats the exact name so ill know what to buy
Samantha	idk its paris hilton ahhahah
Chris	just go with me and ill buy you something too hahahahah
Samantha	id marry you
Chris	november 6th my day off. im down, are you? lmao about the going to buy stuff that is haha
Charlie	I love when girls cuss all the fucking time..........
Samantha	fuck dick cunt bitch nigger ass shit. hey go FUCK yourself
Charlie	Ill take that as a compliment

Drake	When you talk to a girl on FB than meet up with her and your like DAMN BITCH, you must be a photoshop professional of some sort...
Arceli	i knew that's what you were thinking when we met.... dang it.
Drake	Actually it was..

Arceli	well this is awkward.....
Darin	Facebook angles in full effect
Hank	Imagine what they think when they see you Drake.....lol
Bentley	everytime..flawless victory^^

Samantha	maybe i'm just too fucking complicated for anybody to love.

Roel	love isnt complicated
Mason	I haven't had a shot yet ;) bahahaha
Kylie	Me too!
Samantha	you're beautiful and everyone loves you kylie♥
Mason	Oh I don't get a compliment cool :p
Kylie	Aw thanks :3
Samantha	course love♥
Mason	-_- oh how I love you samantha! Not!
Samantha	Tony loves you ...
Mason	Hold on I'm gonna throw up.... Hahaha jk
Jane	No he loves me!
Teddy	maybe your just to special for anyone to love you
Tony	yes i do love you!:)
Samantha	that was actually really clever. Hahah
Kylie	Tony hates me :c
Tony	no i dont:(
Samantha	no he loves you, and no tony you loveMason♥
Jane	No, he doesn't): he loves ME!
Samantha	we know♥
Tony	we ALLLL know♥
Charlnette	my life
Mason	Everyone hates me. I'm not loved :,,,(wah
Samantha	of course♥ and charlnette you're amazing shh♥

Samantha	it's thanksgiving, some people bake pies, but we bake ourselves ♥

Troy	haha ashton kutcher ;)
Troy	lmao^

Deandre	**trying to get a girlfriend, let alone a friend who is a girl without facebook is pretty hard nowadays**
Brittney	**Its so annoying how I only like guys who don't like me a lot at first but when a guy comes around who likes me right from the beginning I get annoyed and uninterested janshsheksnzhdj no wonder I'm single haha I think like a boy -_-**
Stacey	**When you realize that guys like you more when you stop liking them... you're all complicated as fuck!**
Drake	**I'm not sure anything sounds more bitchy than when someone just says "HA"**
Desiree	**I guess its chill to be harrassed by your ex bf.... Grow the hell upppp.**
Kristine	**I'll fight a bitch Xoxo, Gossip girl**
Desiree	**Haha its well needed. Thanks gurl, XOXO**
Kristine	**Hahahhahaloveeeeeyouuubabyyy :)**
Desiree	**Love you tooo baby booo♥**
Darwin	**I'm here for you :)**
Marianne	**Do I need to take care of this?**
Desiree	**Haha I got it thanks though marianne :)**
Marianne	**hahahahah ;p I love you. Don't worry about that mother f*%#*^... You're way better than him.**
Desiree	**Oh trust me I'm well aware :) hahaha douche**
Marianne	**hahahha he's a faggot ♥**
Desiree	**Who's into 14 year olds I guess that's chill.**
Marianne	**People who use girls that can't get pregnant yet cause they haven't had their period :)**
Desiree	**Hahahahaha I love you.**
Marianne	**I FREAKING LOVE YOU ♥**

BURN

Lulu	**I don't hate you, but if you were burning on fire and I had a glass of water I'd drink it :)**
Samantha	**i. fucking. hate. you. stupid. prick.**
Kynsley	**lololololololo fuck you, you suck at lying. gooodnight♥**
Stacey	**Theres plenty of fish in the sea, so back the fuck off my fish.**
Sierra	**funny how this bitch CALLS herself a fuckin pussy and still trys to act like a hardass. dumb biitchh.**
David	**Set up lie detector? Yup fuck the bullshit I'm over it. I swear people who run out of lies for their lies are pathetic**
Linsey	**everyone: shut the fuck up and mind your own business. if you hear something, don't run your big ass mouth about it to someone else, ask me first. k thanks.**
Samantha	**if you actually "cared" about somebody, you wouldn't do such fucked up shit to them all of the time.**
Rebecca	**No, I don't wanna hear about your weekend and how many guys you hooked up with... Bye**

Liam	**You dont like me?..thats cool..fuck you and have a nice day :)**
Kynsley	**when a throw down happens in class at my old school securitys there in a quickness. at my new school you get to watch some little santa claus sub hold back a bitch about to fight a dude. lolololo im dying.**
Rebecca	**When people delete your comment.... Uh bitch I was talking to you.**
Stacey	**Lifes a bitch, oh wait no, that's you.**
Sierra	**biitches think they can slapp a guy cuz they cant do shiit back, heeell naa.**

> Keegan **thank you for being the few females that think that.**
> Sierra **yu kno how it is keegan, SLAP A BITCH**
> Keegan **damnn rightt:P**

Samantha	**now you're just somebody that i used to know.**
Jerran	**You act SO hard on FB, but yet you call me crying? hmmm....stfu.**
Samantha	**cheating with somebody, or on somebody is fucking pathetic haaa.**

> Stanley **agreed**
> Samantha **♥**

Linsey	**rehab is only cool if your 40 and recovering from heroin...fucking love StaceyandSamantha**
Daniel	**why would rehab be cool at all...**
Jeric	**Yeah I went for heroin but I'm not forty so yeah fuck you! (:**
Linsey	**because daniel, it would be an accomplishment. and oh okaayyysowwwy Jeric. Hahahah**
Jeric	**Haha it's chillinhomie!**
Kynsley	**i'm in rehab and i'm 16 and it's an accomplishment for me, so what're you guys trying to imply...**
Jeric	**Your in rehab and they let you have your phone I think not**
Kynsley	**bitch, have you ever heard of outpatient intensive treatmeant? i think not. mind you're own fucking bussniess.**
Daniel	**you go kynsley :D**
Kynsley	**thaanks Daniel ♥**
Jeric	**Uhmm yeah you probley go to the school for losers Hahah.. for marijuana.......**
Kynsley	**definatley not, and for xanax & esctasy smart fuck dont act like you know me or my life.**

Amber	**you know who, pissses me off; she likes all of his status's and everything. Weekend of october 30th, her life ends. We'll show her that she needs to leave other people's property alone, ♥♥♥ :)**
Amethyst	**I have no idea what this is about, but I want in:):)**
Amber	**please do ♥**
Amethyst	**♥**

Brittney	**Stop wearing Uggs with shorts..............**
Jericho	**HAHAHA Brittney ♥**
Greg	**Uggs are ugglies**
Bruce	**I wear uggs with shorts...**
Brittney	**WHY. -_____-**
Peter	**why does it matter some people like it.**

Brittney	**Its so ugly**
Trevor	**its hot**
Peter	**its ugly when girls criticize what other people wear. what difference does it make in yours or anyone else's life**
Gabriel	**HAHAHAHAHA**
Richard	**girls who wear that look like weather-confused sluts just saying**
Peter	**funny, a girl can be a slut for wearing clothes uggs with shorts. Ididntknow**
Brittney	**k bye**
Richard	**i said "look like" not "are"**
Brittney	**apparently i offended Peter because he just posted a status LOL**
Peter	**no its not just you its a group of people. i just think these opinions should be kept personal an not publish for the fact that someone can be offended. not me obviosly but others.**
Brittney	**you're annoying me**
Richard	**it's called a fucking opinion and it's not going to change if someone disagrees with it**
Peter	**cuz i made a good point and you dont want to accept it.**
Peter	**and everyone is entitled to the'r "fucking opinion"**
Brittney	**how did you make a good point? hahahah my "fucking opinion" is that uggs with shorts looks stupid.**
Peter	**but some opinions should be kept personal**
Brittney	**I DON'T GIVE A FUCK**
Brittney	**i doubt anyone's gonna cry because of this status. its not even mean. stop getting all butthurt for other people your a boy you shouldn't be wearing uggs anyways**
Richard	**I agree they should, but if she chooses to say hers, then that's her choice.**
Brittney	**I didn't even say it in a mean way so idk why he's so offended**
Peter	**im not offended at all. i obviously do not wear em cuz i am a boy. and you didnt say it in a mean way but what the fuck does it matter to you if someone else wears that and its not uggs and shorts, that has nothing to do with it. dont critique other people styles cuz u have no right. it isn't your job, and regardless on the severity of the offense the comment**

	shouldnt be said cuz that little bit of offense can change someone's mood.
Richard	Actually she does have a right. Freedom of speech haha
Brittney	shut up Peter...........you obviously are offended because you keep commenting back......hhahhahahahahaha like i seriously don't care
Peter	your right it is her right haha but i misspoke, it is wrong and rude to say so. and sorry if the point i am trying to state contradicts with your opinion. But thats life. everything thought/opinion has a opposing one and you need to realize that and get used to it. I keep commenting because i am trying to get you to understand the cons of posting things like this but you are being stubborn and not wanting to listen and here my thoughts. soi will leave it at that and stop commenting on your status. i intend no hard feelings at all.
Richard	Yeah i guess what he's saying is just know what you're posting could offend someone haha
Brittney	i don't fucking care Peter omg.........I don't give a fuck if people get offended by anything I say. No one is fucking nice to me, ever, so why would I give a fuck if people get offended by shit I say? You're making something so small into some huge ordeal trying to make me feel like shit. I don't. I think uggs with shorts looks stupid. get over it.
Peter	last comment i swear. because you don't get treated nice by some assholes doesn't mean you should treat others like that. I really didn't intend to make you feel bad at all and i apologize if i did. but yeah, Richard that is my point exactly
Brittney	I'm not fucking treating anyone mean shut the fuck up you're annoying the shit out of me leave me the fuck alone. get the fuck over it I DONT GIVE A FUCK
Charles	It does look retarded. And lol @ faggots arguing with brit about fashion on facebook.
Brittney	seriously.
Richard	lol
Andy	Omg guyz calm down plz
Brittney	ha
Richard	hella heated

Peter	im not arguing and watch what the fuck you say charles
Brittney	you were literally just arguing with me.
Peter	i was conversing and putting my point across i had no anger at all in this whole conversation
Brittney	seriously go away.
Peter	okay im done. I didnt mean for this to get out of hand, but to that fuck up there who's trying to kiss your ass, really dude be more educated and respectful than to post a stupid comment like that.
Brittney	BYE
Charles	what are you gonna do try and tell me what to wear? Lmao kid
Peter	no sorry but if you weren't illiterate you would know that i mean the exact opposite of that.
Gabriel	i regret commenting/liking this....so....many....notifications.....
Tori	JUST SO YOU GUYS KNOW. BOYS CAN WEAR UGGS.

Brittney	When guys who graduated two years ago, hit on sophomore and juniors in high school, it really makes me wonder why they can't get with girls their own age...try growing up? Ha. Seriously...
Chris	that hurt lol. because younger girls are more fun.
Brittney	it's also illegal.
Chris	"hit on" means fuck now? Lol
Brittney	Like it's chill if you're FRIENDS with younger girls, but trying to get with them is weird haa.
Justin	^^^^^ most likely...
Brittney	Like if you were a junior or a senior when we were in eighth grade, then that's weird hahaha
Glenyl	I think this all the time.
Brittney	There's like instances where its okay but sometimes it's just weird..hahahah
Chad	but most girls go for guys who are out of high school when their like 15 , 16. they need to grow upppp
Chris	ok Brittney. i graduated early took advanced classes because i had the opportunity. im only 18 so a junior is what? 17? thats so wrong i know huh?

Brittney	It seriously just depends on the situation. I'm talking about 19 and 20 year olds going after 15 and 16 year olds haha. 18 isn't that big of a deal.
Brittney	When you're 19 you'd think you would have moved on to older girls.......
Chad	well idk im only 16 ha! :D
Chris	yepp but in my case I dont think its wrong of me to talk to girls a little younger..like a sophomore or junior. and considering ive never dated a girl "my age" i doubt that'll change
Mitch	David!
Brittney	So am I ha and I've talked to guys who are already graduated but when 19 year olds and 20 year olds try to talk to me and hit on me I straight up ignore them because I think it's weird. Mitch... David's only 18...
Chad	I dont even know him and i hear people say he be creepin hard
Brittney	I like David tho......he'snice..
Roy	he broke into my friends house no hes not
Brittney	Well I'm sorry thats very unfourtunate...why ahah

Brittney	when you see your ex at a party and he has his little girlyfriend scream "fuck youu" out the car..oh my god haahahahashuttuppppp

Jericho	wow dumb bitch hahaha
Tasha	when you see your boyfriends ex and you see her in her car flipping you off because she's pissed that you got what she wanted... oh my god. KEEP IT COMIN ♥
Jericho	lmao
Alyana	What's that? I cunt hear you
Brittney	YOULL NEVER GUESS WHO THE BITCH WAS EITHER! Soooo fucking typical ♥
Claire	Pusssyassexiswear he's soo ugly you're to pretty
Claire	She's got a big schnosee
Brittney	Thank youuu, hahahes immature as fuck even I can break him in half..

Brittney	Yes she does, she doesn't even have a reason to not like me, thats the funny thing. After all the shit she gave me I was STILL nice to her bc I hate drama and it must bother her if she's gonna go outta her way to be a bitch. Immature ass bitches I swear
Claire	I bet. Aha fuck dating twig skinny ugly

Brittney	When guys cuss me out because their girlfriends tell me to, then come back months later after they break up trying to hit on me, fucking pathetic and annoying.

Brittney	BY THE WAY I DO FUCKING REMEMBER YOUR NAMES. Fucking faggots.
Charmie	Hahahaha I love you
Brittney	Love you too ♥
Greg	This is why I'm scared of you...
Richard	fuck you bitch
Brittney	Greg I love you though.. Richard hey
Richard	hey.
Greg	I love you too. But i could still imagine you chopping my arm off if I ever got on your bad side O.o
Brittney	dont piss me off homegurl

Drake	Not all guys want one thing, so everyone can stop posting the same shit all night :)

Kynsley	alright, instead of posting indirect status's to these little freshman, i'ma just say it upfront. FRESHMAN GIRLS STOP TRYING TO BE SLUTS, & MAYBE YOU'LL GET SOME RESPECT COMING YOUR WAY. ♥
Kynsley	except for a few girls, and whoever else is pure at our school in grade 9. :)

162

Trey	and meee!!!!!1
Malou	I was pure in 9th grade ;)
Kynsley	And yoouu trey :) but you're in grade 10! &i know malou, remember Kynsley kiss jess for me, i just wanna see how it goes, HAHAHHAAHHAH *kiss*. AGAIN!
Malou	Hahahahahahyesss:) Im such a little girl!
Kynsley	Muahahaa, iknow ! sheesh, i remember the first words you said to me "your boyfriend thinks i'm beautiful" ahahah in my head i was like "does this bitch know who i am? i will attack her" ahahhahahahahhaahaha.
Malou	Aahahhahahahah, ididnt mean it like that:/ I was literally like a baby ididnt know how to put words together. I feel bad. Ahahahha Love you :)
Kynsley	&ahahaha, i know malou. :)AHAHAH, i was like, uh okay. then i gave him like the death stare across the gym and he saw it too cause he texted me about it, MAUAHAHA
Malou	Aahahahahhahahah we were really immature last year!!no joke!! Ahahahah
Kynsley	haaaaha, i know. :) welli was somewhat mature, now i'm just too serious. ahhaha
Malou	Ahahahha :) Freshman year was ugly.
Kynsley	freshman year, was the shit malou! we didn't have to worry about grades, that's why i fucked up second semester on purpose, now sophomore is gonna kill me, &YOU,
Malou	Really?!Blahh :/ Im just actually gonna try this year.. Like im so confident in it. Like i can get a 3.0 or higher if i wanted i just choose not to. But I will!!! You to!!
Kynsley	Ahahaha, sure you will malou!:) you we're texting me in class during our final... you sit, like five seats away, this report card i'm only gonna have two f's :)
Malou	Hahahahha I know!! Your like " Whats the answers" And im like " Uhh wtf dont ask me im probs the stupidest girl in this class" ahahahahhaha :) Its hard texting in his class:/ AND I WILLLL~!!!!♥
Kynsley	dude, i just got the galaxy i'm not even going to attempt to text at school anymore, the phone is bigger then my hand! ahahhaa, wait whats a gpa, with two f's? i don't think my

	mom will take away my phone, because she knows i suck at mathhhh, ahahahhaha :)
Malou	Ahahahah suckaa. And uhh depends what your other grades are. Tell me your other grades and ill calculate it ;) My mom gave up on me:/ bahahahaAAHAHHAHA JK Im gonna hide my report card. Oh and the song right above it by lil wayne reminds me of us cause were so bad assss :)
Kynsley	GIRL THEY MAIL REPORT CARDS TO YOU.
Malou	ahahahahhahahah :) you're gonna die, how many classes are you failing?
Kynsley	&muahahaha, hells no!, hmm, leemelisteen (; we are badass malou, sheesh.
Kynsley	i do love this song, :)
Malou	Ahahhaha, GIRL I KNOW, ITS CALLED TELLING YOUR PARENTS YOU HAVE TO CHECK THE MAIL AND GET IT. Uhh, like 2 I think.. The rest are A's and Bs. But still:/ And i know meeetooozzz.
Stacey	im not a sluutt :) e
Kynsley	& i'm keri hilson. we both wish these statements were true, but they never will be ♥mauahah

---

Stacey	when did our school become an episode of degrassi? Lol
Velvet	Wow why do so many people like your status?

Drake	I figured it out! Girls like to be treated like shit, and go for assholes because that means they will have something to post on facebook about for the next few weeks :)

Liam	When I go out to eat and see a couple sitting together and one of them is on their phone...get the fuck off your phone haha
Asher	Dude I fuckin hate that shit.

Liam	I just feel bad for the person not using their phone cuz they are getting shut down haha
Asher	Dude I know. Like if you're hanging out with someone and they're texting you feel like you're boring and shit and feel like they don't even wanna be there. Hahaha
Liam	Hahaha exactly! I've been on both ends of that haha

Drake	If you want a boyfriend/girlfriend so bad, stop bitching about it, get off facebook, and go do something about it, no one feels sorry for you.
Jhong	70 likes awaiting..
Maxxwel	eHarmony.
Drake	Fuckbook.com
Rupert	I made it 70 likes:D just so she would be right
Beigel	more likes!

SLUTS & HOES

Linsey	**D.T.F**

Drake	**You can't shake the whore tree and expect an angel to fall out**
Liela	**your annoying. shut up.**
Drake	**Don't get mad at me that everyone shakes your tree and gets disappointed when you fall out**

Stephan	**Dear whores of the Internet Theres something called a diary. Please buy one and stop posting your problems on my newsfeed**
Brittney	**NO**

Samantha	**your vagina is probably like a fucking hallway.**
Isaac	**used daily ? lol**
Samantha	**and very wide.**
Sammy	**...**
Jobim	**Yummy**

Jerome	**Please stop sending me naked pics you slut!**
Kailyn	**awk I thought I was sending them to Wilbur**
Jerome	**well if your gonna send anymore... wear those sluty boots ;)**
Kailyn	**ohhhh ya. n00dz &b00tz ya**
Jerome	**:)♥**

Samantha	you just throw your cat at just about anybody don't you, dumb slut.
Irene	yah the dumb bitch is guna get the shit beaten out of her the day i get back i fucking swear.
Samantha	I'll video tape it ♥ love you
Irene	love yu bestfriend!

Rylie	Personally, I think the word "slut is used to lightly to describe someone. Flirt's aren't sluts. sluts are people that sleep around, she's a virgin, so how does that make her a slut? Just someone you don't like, doesn't make them a slut.
Carlo	you go girl!
Rylie	for you boo.
Erika	Rylie, your a slut.
Rylie	hmm am I now?
Erika	Heckkkkkaaa
Rylie	hummies 4 lyf!
Beverly	every girl who attends high school should take your advice because that seems to be the only word they know
Rylie	Exactly.

Kynsley	twinkle, twinkle little whore. close your legs, they're not a door (;
Christa	i love it ♥
Kynsley	tehehehe (;
Marlou	lol
Junie	wow kynsley....haha
Herbert	hahaha this status made my day

Samantha	the problem with you is you feel fucking obligated to have sex with any guy who gives you some sort of attention and then you

wonder why they never like you back..? you didn't even let them chase you, you gave it up in a heartbeat.

Drake   you post pictures bending over, talk like a slut and party like a rockstar, yet you wonder why you cant find your man...

Carmen   Ayyyy yo, all dem single boyz looking for single ladies should hit me and my main betch up with a sext(; we only want you if your ding dong is bigger den a baby carrot. get @ us.— withRowena.

Rowena	g3t @ u$ ♥
Lily	what about the same as a baby carrot?
Lilibeth	Hahahahah no baby carrots(;
Willard	I have a big black penis.
Lily	aww :/
Daniel	Shit Im out then...
Sidney	Wtf
Rowena	Sorry Daniel (;
Lilibeth	So many small weenies in this town!
Daniel	But hey the fact you ignore me puts me out too
Rowena	What?
Daniel	Is that to me?
Rowena	Yess
Oliver	Good thing I don't have an asian penis :)
Daniel	Look at the messages with us, see how much you reply:....
Rowena	:(
Daniel	Is that to me?
Oliver	Ok
Oliver	Mines an inch bigger than a baby carrot haha Jkjk
Oliver	It two inches bigger haha
Rowena	L o l
Daniel	This is to confusing
Ezekiel	Mine is the size of a banana:)
Willard	bananas come in various sizes homie, got be specific when hollering at ladies of this caliber.

Ezekiel	#Petitebanana
Oliver	It's the small green bananas
Willard	well that's unfortunate...
Oliver	Oh well ya for asians
Willard	good thing I have a black penis and not an Asian one..
Elijah	Mines as big a Willard hahaha
Elijah	*as
Oliver	Mines bigger than the empire state building
Willard	I dick slapped Pluto out of our solar system..
Rowena	We dont want anyone anymore..these notifications are annoying ♥ mwahh.
Oliver	Damn I dick slapped..... Ummm ummm ..... I got nothin you won this round
Oliver	Hey friend request me
Elliott	fosho.
Rufus	lol

Franklin	Hey baby I love u!!! That girl didn't deserve u!!! She's a hoe!!!
Sherwin	Hahaha what girl? I already forgot?
Franklin	Haha um... She was a blonde... About 5 ft whore
Pearl	It would be nice if you didn't talk shit on my bestfriend. Thanks
Franklin	It be nice if your bestfriend didn't cheat on my bestfriend & play him and get back with him then break up with him or her ex
Sherwin	Hahahahahahahaha
Pearl	Haha too bad you did the same exact thing Franklin mhmm.. Weird. Talk shit when you have room to talk. Lol
Sherwin	Haha this isn't about Franklin. Ha Amira fucked up she knows it... Even if she doesn't want to admit it she knows
Franklin	Weird how people make mistakes. I owned up to mine.. I'm back with Mariphel and were happy... I didnt play her either and I never lied to her. I also didn't say I was In love with her and lie about it. Also didn't go behind her back and text a bunch of girla

Pearl	she's not a whore. End of story.
Sherwin	Pearl you prob shunt say anything else I know she is your best friend and you want to defend her but she fucked up and it's over now like we both he talked moved on and she is with someone. It's all good just don't drag by best friends into it
Sherwin	My *
Arnel	Why u so butt hurt dood I thought u didn't care?? Haha yall are bunch of clowns
Franklin	Arnel seriously get the fuck out. This convo is over no one does care anymore.
Franklin	Stop talking shit Amira already got mad at Sherwin for sayin shit to you cuz u showed her the messages like a little bitch so jus stop u look like an idiot
Sherwin	Haha funny shit Arnel you need to stop seriously no one cares u didn't even need to comment on this.
Arnel	Obviously yall do
Sherwin	Stop saying yall you sound like an idiot and what ever think what you wan late
Amelia	Sherwin and Franklin stop talking to these idiots :) you guys shouldnt waste your time on these people
Jocelyn	I agree :) Sherwin and Franklin are way too good to even talk to this child Arnel or whatever hahahahahaSherwin and Franklin... Enjoy your senior year you guys are both stars on the baseball team and are going to be in college very soon and going far in baseball :) let this little kid enjoy his moment he feels he's getting right now. You two have a LOT more going for you guys :) loveeee both brothers!
Amira	Hahaha just to let Y'ALL know Arnel graduated early an he's goin pro in motocross haha so, so much for him having nothing going for him!
Pearl	I only comment on this because of Franklin talking shit on my bestfriend being childish so that doesn't make me a idiot.
Jocelyn	Haha oh my god. HAHAHAHA
Amelia	baseball players > motorcross riders. sorry bout it
Jocelyn	^^^^ agreeAnd I also wish I had a dollar for everytime I heard a guy say he was going "pro" in motorcross or his girlfriend saying that because I'd be so rich

Jocelyn	**And baseball players > motorcross riders**
	Sorry I'm NOT sorry ha

Samantha	**stop asking for a good girl, when you're chasing hoes.**
Javier	**Stop asking for a good man and letting dick heads beat up the guts.**
Samantha	**Touché.**
Billy	**EXACTLY^^^^^^^^^^**

Easton	**Kiss me like you miss me. Fuck me like you hate me.**

Samantha	**I hope you drown in all the cum you fucking swallow.**
Anthony	**god im sorry): </3**
Rowena	**This makes me sick..**
Samantha	**ahahah yum**
Trina	**hhahaha yessss!**
Colt	**jesus....**
Ringgold	**tf?**
Samantha	**...like she's a head slut and swallows a lot of semen....**
Luis	**omg i love that song**
Samantha	**I don't think it's a song though.**
Luis	**no no it is.. thats the exact lyric..**
	http://www.youtube.com/watch?v=Ky3mhBzaDBA
	its like the 3rd or 4th line
Daniel	**I was about to say that luis!!!**
Jestone	**god damn I hope you never get pissed at me hahaha**
Ulric	**Damn!**

Samantha	**I've come to the realization that our generation is so fucked up beyond repair. Girls have had sex with more people in one night,**

than somebody has had in their whole lifetime...like that's just not right.

Pinky	if a girl has had sex with only one guy then technically thats still gonna be more than somebody has had sex with in their entire life because alot of people haven't had sex haha
Tasha	Yes ^
Jasmine	Let's all be virgins.
Samantha	I'm talking about girls who have sex with like three people in one night....
Pinky	oh haha i knew that, i just wanted to get clever with it
Samantha	ahah yeah♥ you had a good point
Tasha	Who in the fuck does that -_-
Jasmine	Sluts?
Tasha	Not really. I've never heard of a girl fucking 3 guys in ONE night but ohhhh K
Samantha	ahah half of Town High School
Jasmine	Shit happens.
Pinky	yeah never been to a party where thats happened either in the past 18 years lol
Tasha	You happened
Samantha	No but really I know like three girls who have done it and it's super sad. Hahaah
Mark	Ive seen it i think four guys hahah
Pinky	dang it shouldve been headline news! haha and people used to call me a slut? never done something like that
Samantha	you're not a slut♥ hah
Pinky	awhhh thanks(: hahahaa
Samantha	Love ♥
Shawn	Sex
Darius	lawl 3 people in one night wonder who your talking about;)
Samantha	bye slut
Samantha	K bye darius
Darius	what?
Rowena	Hehehehe i know who this is (;
Darius	me too, thats why im confused why she said k bye darius

Samantha	ahhaah everybody knows(; and I thought you were like being mean ahahah
Jomer	Bada ba da imlovin it
Darius	no haha i just was saying i know who your talking about

---

Brittney	That one guy who hits on every single underage girl in Town via Facebook then talks about all the pussy he gets........if you really had that much game you wouldn't have to use a computer......*sighh*

Mitch	once again David!
Brittney	hey she's a nice lady!
Carl	:(
Jonard	BLESSTHISFUKNPOST_
Brittney	hahaha<33
Rylie	LOLOLOLOLOLOLOLOLOL.
Brittney	wut
Rylie	what mitch said
Dindo	Creepers.
Brittney	baby
Dindo	Hi Brittney.
Brittney	itexted your sexyass this morning and you didn't replyy
Charles	Probably hittin up all the desperate undercover hoes lmao
Brittney	Yeaaaaaaaaaaaaaaaaaahhh...no.
Charles	Well you wouldn't get classy women that way lols
Brittney	Nowhere in this status did I say it worked...
Charles	hitting up doesn't mean it's working, just that he's trying.
Brittney	oh my god stop go away goodbye
Charles	reading doesn't go away
Brittney	bye
Charles	lol u mad
Brittney	No you're being annoying so I'm dismissing you
Charles	well. people who can't read annoy me too, but I don't throw a fit lmao
Brittney	I'm not throwing a fit. I can read, obviously. Go away.
Charles	not when you interpret something wrong

Brittney	**FUCK OFF OH MY FUCKING GOD**
Charles	**just block me if it bothers you that much little lady**
Brittney	**You're so fucking annoying**
Charles	**then do something about it jesuschrist do you have brain damage?**
Brittney	**ya**
David	**555-5555 who wants to meet up? I wouldn't mind fuxking some little pussysup**
David	**@mitch and Rylie**
Brittney	**David shush ha**
Aaron	**Mitch Rylie . they're tagged now hahaha**
Brittney	**hahahahahgoddammit..**
Rylie	**what's this going to prove? I just thought what he said was funny, doesn't mean I agreed with him. Your just making yourself look childish calling me out on a facebbokstatus.**
Empress	**once again, trying to fuck little pussys... o.O**
Brittney	**Hahahahahgoddammit**
David	**Jahahahaha well my numbers right there fuck all of you haters makin me famous I'll throw down idgaf what's good**
Brittney	**Stopppppppppppppppppppphahahaha**
Xian	**spitting game on the computer is the only way to do it... you should have seen mine conversation with the 8th grader last week;)**
Brittney	**mm baby ;)**
Mitch	**DAVID IS SO HARD OMG**
Tanner	**Sketchhhhhhhhhhh**

Samantha	**fuck all the hoes my niggas blow treeeeeeeeees ;)**
Elton	**Ok fasho i digg it**

Stacey	**Girls are aloud to dress like sluts on Halloween, I don't want to here anything else about it. K.**

Stephan	Alot of girls dress like sluts everyday Halloween is just an exception to be super sluty so don't expect anyone to cut you girls a brake(:
Stacey	Girls that dress like sluts everyday, get absolutely noo respect from me ha.

Drake	And she thinks I'm wrong for calling her a slut a month ago..
Joshua	That has to be staged haha.
Milton	what the fuck ..
Drake	No she's literally a slut. She always takes pics of her "abs" but she will have panties on or something. Shes fucking stupid she got really butthurt about a month ago when I commented in her pic calling her a slut.
Joshua	This girl seems like the kind of person who would have thousands of subscribers even though she's not famous haha
Creighton	Hahahahahahahahahahahahahahaha. I hope the piercing is like dipped in STD juice... (if thats possible)
Drake	I hope they use a staple gun and accidentally staple her vagina shut
Creighton	Hahahahahahaha staple it lol. They have colorful staples! It would be convenient
Maribel	That's classy.. Not
Ricky	Dude... Grody....
Joshua	I can never understand where the motivation comes to do something like that?
Douglas	Girls seriously amaze me more and more everyday
Ricky	Give somebody a reason to be down there. Obviously guys like us got smart and realized its unclean. Hahahaha
Leizel	I would rather get my head and eyebrows shaved and get both of my legs broken by a stampeed of elephants , before I get my clit pierced ..
Ricky	Win^

Creighton	The funny part is,
	She's worried about riding a horse...
Drake	I got dared to let a donkey nibble on my peanut butter covered nipples while dipping my balls in boiling water, how bad will this hurt? Will the pain last more than a week?
Tyrone	She updates her facebook like 27 times in 27 mins, i deleted her hahaha
Creighton	Hahahahah.
Ricky	Well Drake. If you hadnt added every girl in the know universe you wouldnt have to deal with her hahaha
Drake	This one added me!
Connie	she's nice
Whitney	Girl that posts 20 statuses a day?
Pat	I went to high school with her, she was really annoying and I drew on her sweatshirt, she was a little upset about it hahahaha.
Barry	very mature calling someone a slut, just leave her be haha
Beigel	That's what's up ^^

Samantha	people have no fucking standards my god.

Stacey	Here's to the girls that refuse to be distasteful and sluty to get a guys attention. The world needs more of you.

Stacey	I'm a dirty slut
Amanda	its okay im a dirty skank haha
Rylie	Lolwut?
Tim	someones coming out.....& Rylie you lying son of a dickhole, you said you had work at 2.....
Rylie	I'm on my lunch, eat cock. And I will always love Stacey as my sister
Tim	you eatinng cock, that makes you a dirty slult!
Rylie	I told you to eat cock.

Tim	just shutup fool! hhahah
Jonathan	haha fags ^
Rylie	Look who's talking -___-
Enrique	Oh definately
Mario	yes you are :)
Chloe	me too ;)
Stacey	Hahaha people like to hack my Facebook but hella slut

Tristan	Doing me!! let hoes be hoes I guess....
Tina	Awwww, that doesn't sound good...lol...
Yael	love you Tristan!!! ;)
Yna	Tristan dont blame ya my son says theres no good girls out there anymore...but a lots of hoes.
Lloyd	Was it really necessary to call her like 15-20 times everyday? I was with her all last week so just wondering...
Tristan	deff not talking about her she's not a hoe well maybe idkhaha and I was just screwing with her cuz she's pretty immature
Lloyd	Right on. Didn't know the mature thing to do was call someone 20 times a day.
Clifford	Haters mannn
Tristan	idk it was that many times but like I said I was screwing with her and any ways who the freak are you get off my status!
Bryle	aahaa
Lloyd	Get your status off my news feed niggaaa
Clifford	If you dont want him on your news feed then delete him and jump off his status that simple damn highschool drama lol
Tristan	delete me buddy! ahahah you're a idiot!
Tristan	true that clifford thanks bud lollil boy trying to act hard for his girl
Lloyd	Tristan, dude, shut up talking about me. I had nothing to do with this and he's not trying to act hard for his girl because we aren't like that. My god. Both of you stop.
Daisy	Ohh Tristan...haters are gonna hate...you're better than them... keep doin you bud ;)

Lloyd	And thanks for clearing it up that I'm not the hoe hah but I'm not immature either so both of y'all just needahushhhhh

---

Drake	I honestly think it's ridiculous how every girl complains about being fucked over and just wants to find that nice guy who's good to her, yet she fucks that nice guy over... Make up your fuckin mind...
Maxwell	bipolar emotions.
Rose	Umm.. Most guys complain ALL the time about there not being enough good girls and being fucked over too.
Melinda	dumb hoes ... smh
Alfred	Drake is right
Reynald	then they get back with the douche, and the cycle begins again.
Rose	Dude, seriously? Stop blaming girls for everything. You "guys" are 50% of the problem.
Hermie	hahaha. girls are fake as fuck and hoes and guys are hoes but too real for the girls too handle.
Maxwell	I mean I guess we could all be gay ..
Hermie	girls should just go lesbian instead of complaining alllllllltheeefuckingggtimeee
Rose	Holy fuck. If I got a penny for every time a guy complained, I'd be throwin change at hoes all day long!
Joshua	Girls like to complain about their life so they can get some attention. But in reality, they like to be treated like crap because that presents a challenge for them. Once they think they have you and that they don't have to work to keep you around. They'll always be unfaithful, or will just move on.
Gina	turn gay.
Benedict	bitches are bitches, cant do nothin about it.
Mardy	Not all girls are like that, just like how not all guys are bad. Just sayin'.
Kenneth	BITCHES AIN'T SHIT BUT HOES &TRICKS, jusssayin' ...

Dennis	Only time of the year that all the girls get to dress up as hoe's and not get crap for it. Congratulations would you like a cookie?
Tara	I had a cookie this morning
Jude	The true sluts come out on Halloween cause all they wear is underwear

---

Brittney	Samantha is a whore cuz she sends me naked pictures all day evrryday..andi love it <696969 text me! 555-5555
Samantha	and i wear the bombshell ;)
Brittney	I wear two ;)
Brittney	It really does dude...hahaha
Samantha	hahahahah it really does
Brittney	Hahahaha get one dude!!!!
Brittney	I wear them..haha
Samantha	oh you little fake bitch
Brittney	Im so faaaake omg ;) text me back......... -_-

Brittney	If you know someone is already taken, respect their relationship.. don't be the reason they end up single. Dumb bitches.
Brittney	You aintnuttinbuttahoocie mama! Hoodrathoodrathoociemama!
Randy	Yea dumb putas
Cameron	amen!
Brittney	Hahahahahahahahhahahahhahahaim laughing so hard..
Cameron	yeah.!
Brittney	Love you too! Lets chilllllaxxx soon k
Rustom	fuck yea
Brittney	Rustom this about you...you skank
Ara	Hahah I feel creepy cause I like almost every one of your status'... but its cause they're true. Haha
Rustom	heyyhaha

Brittney	**Lets have a toast for the douchebags, lets have a toast for the assholes, lets have a toast for the scumbags everyone of them that i know**

Brittney	**Hahahaha :)**
McKenzie	**woahi was going to say that but that fucker said it before me.**
Brittney	**God DAMNIT mckenzie your fuckinup!!!**
Brittney	**Fuck...this is embarrassing**
McKenzie	**its okay! You just beat me to it, and i respect you for that. Yeah brittney....you illiterate fuck**
Piyush	**i was JUST listening to thtsong**
Brittney	**Now im crying thanks. Perez hiltons real name is mario... marinate on that mckenzie**
Brittney	**Yes so was i**
McKenzie	**whawhawhaaaaaaat. My life just turned upside down....you cant just lay such fat news on me without a warning brittney!**

Brittney	**I <3 douchebags 555-5555**

Eli	**I love them too they amaze me.**
Brittney	**Douchebags!?**
Eli	**yeah fasho! just kidding fuck douchebags.**
Brittney	**Your not one are you!?**
Eli	**nope:)**
Brittney	**AW yay :) haha**
Eli	**haha. I think I've talked/texted you before....like a few months back. I'm not sure though....**
Brittney	**I dont think so or id havce your numvberstillll! I save every number**
Eli	**I didn't save it either...I'll text you right now though. what's your # ?**
Brittney	**555-5555 :)**
Eli	**I texted you:)**

Brittney	Does hearing about a girls trashiness just go over guys' heads? I don't gett how trashy girls get hot guyyyssssdusgfbweugtentiw4rt! !!!!!gjdn ugh
Jenelyn	haters gonnahate
Brittney	what
Jenelyn	u lmao
Brittney	oh uhm ok. i get to see you in like 2 days......
Jenelyn	ill see u in 30 something hours
Brittney	get stoked rite aid!?>
Jenelyn	ishinkkkshoi might go to the front bitch ill let u know thoo tomorrow night....
Brittney	you better wait for me.............
Bea	Because they know they will get laid... lol.. That's all sluts are good for. x)
Charlie	Right on the dot ^
Brittney	gay as fuck
Alyana	Seriously my thoughts these past few days. Like why do boys keep hooking up with ugly sluts? They're dirty

Brittney	Why don't you go put on some clothes, take a non-slutty picture, then go do a swan dive off a fucking cliff...dumb whore.
Trey	i'd rather pencil dive
Rhanel	so much anger Brittney....chilllaaaxxxxxxbrahhh whatever floats your boat cat ppooop Rhanel i hate everyone k
Rhanel	...not me :)
Brittney	hahahahahhahahahah this is more toward girls Rhanel hahahi know seriously
Melissa	sdflkashglkhdhlks. I LOVE YOUOUYO$Y
Brittney	hahahahi love you too (:
Katrina	HAHAHHAAHAHAH. omgthatsgreat.
Stephanie	swan dive= style points
Brittney	If your gonna go at least go in style
Stephanie	watch and you will pee your pants

Andy	this is greaaaaat hahaha
Brittney	What can isayyyyy :Dhahaha
Stephanie	psh if you want style go off the cliff in a tutu eating a burrito listening to dubstep. Thatsstyle
Julia	HAHAHA i love this<3333

Linsey	boys wear the pants in the relationship but girls control the zipper;)

Joe	Keep thinkin that ;)
Linsey	its trueeeee! or at least i always do (:
Joe	Well good for you! :)
Brent	but babe i got basketball shorts on so what now ha
Linsey	now i hate you. justkiddding. thats fine babe coz im boss anyways;)
Brent	ha ha you wish baby
Linsey	know* not wish. just admit it.
Joe	You tell him Linsey
Linsey	:)ahahah oh i do, but he never listens/:
Brent	what!
Linsey	♥
Brent	na im not talking to you babe but na you listen to me what are you talkin about ha ha
Linsey	oh welllitsssokay Joe is my friend♥ and iwasnt saying that, i was saying how you dont listen to me !
Brent	i know idont ha jk
Linsey	you really donttho :(
Brent	cause im a g babe ha
Linsey	ahhaahahi hate you kbye</3
Brent	my shit bang lol
Linsey	whaaaat?.
Brent	post lol
Linsey	ohhhi love e-40 :)
Brent	now check out my new post ha ha
Linsey	i did :) i liked ittt
Brent	the new new one ha by love rance and big sean

Samantha	why are the cutest guys such douchebags...
Robert	cute*
Miranda	because i hate life
Samantha	hahhaha
Tony	Jane why'd you like this...-.-
Samantha	your a slut it doesnt matter
Tony	mhmm(;
Samantha	JANE THINKS YOUR A CUTE DOUCHEBAG THATS WHY
Tony	woah there dont be mean now
Samantha	okay douchebag...jk love you bff
Dick	:)
Samantha	douchebag...
Samantha	♥
Dick	Wow.im mad at you...
Samantha	i mean ugly and nice....or cute and a douchebag...
Dick	Im ugly and nice
Raymart	Same goes for girls...
Samantha	hahah oh fine
Samantha	girls are sluts so it doesnt really matter......if they're ugly or cute or nice or mean cause guys will still get pussy hahaha
Raymart	Hahaha are you saying that for all girls?
Samantha	nope just sluts.+
Jane	Oh, just saw this & it's because I think you're a cute dochebag of course (:
Tony	awww thanks love:) and i got lazy and didnt make skype yet yet but i'll do it when i'm done with my essay!:)
Raymart	Ha yeah....
Jane	kaykaykay slut
Rodel	i ask my self that everyday...
Arman	im ugly but i no douche bag
Trey	sorry i try not to be!:(
Trey	;)
Samantha	ahhah shut up husband
Harold	I'm an ugly douchebag :/
Lucky	No
Samantha	i hate all of you

Trey	**love you**
Trey	**<333337**
Samantha	**love you more <//33//3/33383833737377373**
Trey	**k let's go fuck and make babies..**
Samantha	**and abort them all...**
Trey	**except for one:))**
David	**I'm falsly accused as being a douche because I get at all the bitches haha**
Samantha	**♥**
Trey	**david i'm quoting you on that cause it's true and fuckin hilarious**
David	**Haha it's nuts dude the little hoes love the dick but hate when I don't wanna ask them out so I get put on blast by everyone**
Samantha	**hahawhahaha oh my god**
David	**Haha I speak the truth!**
Samantha	**its true and realllllllly sad cause girls are grimy hahaha**
Trey	**people get all butthurt. seriuously david you knows whats up**
Samantha	**you knows**
David	**Dude I love you guys. May my dick stay strong! Pray for me!!!**
Jason	**hahaha**

Kailyn	**Hi, I'm not hitting on your boyfriend. I'm just a nice person, you can back the fuck up now**
David	**Bitches be trippen**
Kailyn	**seriously omfg. "She posted on his wall when he like her status for a post, look at those hearts, look at those winky faces, she's tryna fuck him" nawh bitch gtfo.**
Barbara	**story of my life... so annoying.**
David	**Punch her boobs**
Kailyn	**it's okay, she's already ugly, no need to kick her while shes down.**

Samantha	**you can't have fucking everybody, choose one boy and fucking stick to him stupid slut.**

184

STD'S

Eli	**I dedicate this song to my School.**

	www.youtube.com
	I've Got The Clap (Official Music Video)
Melissa	**#realtalktho**
Tanner	**#clappin**
Eli	**People at that school fucking disgust me. If you know you have chlamydia don't hook up with people.**
Owen	**#real shit**
Melissa	**Seriously............**
Steve	**#This is exactly what happens when no one can control themselves and has sex with all the same people everyone else does**
Eli	**#remembe that day in your car when we were trying to Figure out who the source of Chlamydia was?**
Eli	**#well we know who it is lol**
Brittney	**cant breathe**
Steve	**#hahaha omg yes I do cause it was like 30 people who all had sex with each other and it was really gross cause eventually everyone is going to die because everyone is a scandalous sex addict that need to learn to control their WHOREmones.**
Brittney	**#whos got the clap?**
	#ido! ido!
Eli	**#who likes hash tags?**
Eli	**#we do we do!**
Steve	**#hashtag#**
Paige	**hahahahahahahahahahahaha**

Bernard	yum
	Its embarassing how this is spreading like fucking wild fire.... the few people who have it need to do one of two things.... preferably both get fucking treated and stop having sex with all of the school
Oscar	lol so many status's about STDs this is fucking hilarious

---

| Stacey | P.s you guys didnt "fuck up" my life, you simply gave me a chance to clear out all the std ridden clutter :) |

| Isabel | I thought you were chill & shit, but honestly, fuck you. I hope you get AIDs-_- |
| | K HAVE A NICE LIFE. BYEEE :) |

| Kynsley | *chlamydiabook. i'm going back to myspace. |

| Miley | I would appreciate it if people would stop thinking I have an STD. Its really getting old! |

| Jane | When you still fuck with a bitch that has chlamydia, that's when I say goodbye, you're as dirty as they come ♥ |

Roel	ewww
Jane	That's what I'm saying.
Roel	thats just fuckin nasty
Tony	oh my god not true ahahahaha
Angeline	yes it is Tony.
Jane	^ agreed.
Roel	she's talkin bout u? lmao whostellin the truth here ha
Jane	I am.....

Tony	ehhhhkinda half and half....the chlamidia shits a rumor but i guess since i kissed her when you told me to go hook up with someone that means im dirty as they come♥
Jane	At least you know it ♥ now go away
Angeline	♥ you two were the cutest couple. Tony. tisk.
Jane	Aww, thanks ♥ but sluts will be sluts (:
Roel	hmmm well hook up with people that are clean and rumors suck balls enough with the hearts too lol cant take the convo seriously
Angeline	♥.............. sorry :) i had to
Roel	hahaha♥♥ they are dirty std hearts
Jane	♥♥♥♥♥
Tony	ahahaha alright peace
Roel	ahhh we all have stds now damn hearts
Hazel	so u kissed her while she was with Salvador? U know her BOYFRIEND that she is supposed to be loyal to?!
Angeline	Do you know salvadors girlfriend? It's a mini rae Hazel
Hazel	Hahai know who his girlfriend is supposed to be. Linsey right?
Hazel	well if shes kissing Tony then she is a shitty girlfriend
Roel	woah mas drama
Hazel	LOL you bet theres gonna be drama if shes cheating on my best friend
Roel	so whos cheating on who lol
Hazel	well shes cheating on salvador if she is kissing Tony which mean Tony cheated on Jane.
Jane	Tony & I aren't going out... so he's not technically cheating on me, but he fucked me over... once again (:
Roel	its a cheating circle
Brittney	dacatzouttada bag guise
Hazel	her cat HAS BEEN out and about for a while
Jane	HAHAHHAHAHAHA, omfg
Roel	lol crazy stuff in our Town

Linsey	oh and btw bitches, I don't have chlamydia if you were wondering. hahah. I already got tested but for all you guys who still don't believe me, Eli is taking me again soon and I'm gonna take a video of the doctor saying I don't have it k ♥
Linsey	Hahaha I love you most ♥ Fuck everyone elseeee.
Eli	Linsey get on IM if you can i need to talk to you
Taylor	wtf?
Linsey	Eli text me.
Miles	Hahaha. I hate everyone
Sharon	People are just so ignorant. I love you beautiful!
Jane	sorry for believing it for a minute. love you ♥
Austin	better hope the doctor says you don't
David	If anyone asks me if I have it in person. I'm going to knock them the fuck out. These rumors are so annoyinggggg
Linsey	I've already gotten checked once Austin :) I'm just going again so I can get proof. Miles, we're on the same boat! Ahahah And Jane I fucking love you Sharon, thank you so much gorgeous, love you! And David, I know riiight! I agreeee!
Austin	okay well I hope your clean
David	Austin dont be spreading shit either
Linsey	And yes Austin I am :)
Austin	I'm keepin my dick to myself David
Austin	wait that's not what you mean is it ?
Miles	Linsey call me back ass hole!
Linsey	I will! Hold on, I'm talking to my dadddd. Ahahah
Miles	Hah k
Donald	Y even go out of your way to prove to the public something personal? You don't have anything to prove, just immature kids start drama- its part of life
Linsey	Ahaha that's trueee♥ Thanks donald :) Message me. I misssyou!, I haven't talked to you in foreveerrr.
Penelope	Y should you need to be getting checked?
Linsey	Coz everyone says I have it so I wanna prove I don't have it to the world. But honestly, I dgaf now Penelope. I'm done with all this shiit.
Miles	Linsey your better than that delete it. Not worth the fight

Penelope	Everyone can think what they want but you shouldn't have even have had to get checked in the first place...
Linsey	You're right Miles ♥ love youu. Text me
Miles	Kayy
Linsey	I got checked becoz I thought it was a good idea coz I was scared that I might have gotten something. Its not a bad thing to just check.
Penelope	At this young of age no u shouldn't have too
Clint	Linsey who cares what people sayy you have nothing to prove if u know u don't have it then u don't have to go to the doctor and record its a waste of time people have no lives and say stupid things ignore them
Miles	^ at this age you definitely should...
Linsey	Penelope, I really don't need you playing mommy and telling me I'm too young to check for an std k.
Penelope	I sware you kids start out younger and younger.... I'm disappointed
Linsey	And Clint you are right ♥ I love you. Text me. We never talk anymore :(
Linsey	Uhm I don't really care to be honest? Its my decision. You're only like a year or 2 older than me soooo....?
Penelope	Okay sorry not worried about you worried about my best friend now k
Hilda	I know I don't even live in this Town anymore, but no one should have to deal with the shit you're dealing with. I'm so sorry. People are going to talk no matter what, you shouldn't have to prove anything to anyone. In three years none of this will even matter, who cares what stupid teenagers in Town think of you. Stay strong and keep your head up. Rumors are for children and if kids in high school still believe in rumors, then I feel embarrassed for them, just shows how immature people at your school are for caring so much about your problems.
Linsey	I don't have an std. So just stop right there. I care about salvador a lot. And he knows that. And I like that you're there for him, but he's my boyfriend and you're not apart of mine and his relationshipp so I'd appriciate it if you stayed out of it

	with telling me that I'm too young to check for an std. Better to be safe than be sorrry.
Linsey	Hilda you just made my fucking life. Thank you so much. That means a lot to me to hear you say that. And you're completelyyyy right about everything. I wish more people at school were like you. You're a sweetheart. And honestly tho, I'm not even concerned about all these other bitches at school, all I care about it my relationships with my close friends and my boyfriend. So you're riight, I should even be trippin on what anyone else thinks.
Hilda	Good for you. This stupid rumor will be forgotten in no time :) Just stay strong. Miss ya girl.
Linsey	Hopefully ♥ I miss you tooo. I'm always here for you btw, if you ever need anything. I know we were never that close, but you're so sweet and I wish I would've actually gotten to know you while you lived here! I hope all is going good for you tho♥
Herbert	you dont have it haha people are dumb.
David	Hey Linsey I'm down to just start putting people on blast in person. If they wanna disrespect and spread some fucked up shitlt about something as serious and personal as that is. So here it is to everyone that reads this, If I find out your still spreading these rumors you better be able to take a punch. K and that's all :) aha
David	To all the guys that is
Linsey	Exactllyyy Herbert, love you ♥ And David I fucking adore you. Text me.
Drake	Whats wrong with Chlamydia?
David	Dang for reals right now Drake

| Bobby | CUM in my LYDIA |

| Eli | I retract all previous statements I've said about this chlamydia issue. It's definitely a rumor. |

| Melissa | lets make a chlmydia chart tmorrow so we can figure out who all has it. |

Brittney	**YES YOURE A GENIUS**
Melissa	**YES LUNCH TOMORROW THATS WHAT WE HAVE TO DO**

Brittney	**I was a woman possessed. I spent about 80% of my time talking about Chlamydia, and the other 20% of the time, I was praying for someone else to bring it up so I could talk about it more... I could hear people getting bored with me, but I couldn't stop. It just kept coming up like word vomit.....**
Greg	**Chlamydia is the new black.**
Dindo	**No, wait. Actual vomit**
Brittney	**I'm in love with you**
Dindo	**♥ sext me**

Rowena	**hahahahaha stay classy (;**
Elijah	**Like that's gonna happen hahhaha**
Rowena	**Hahahaha i knoww, its not im not saying im classsy or anythingg, im jussayin our schoool is fucking nasty.**
Elijah	**Yes it is**
Serge	**thats like the pot calling the kettle black. HAHAHA**

Richard	**Not having Chlamydia**

David	**When your so sick you literally think u might die or have some disease or some shit :/**

Stacey	**ahahahahhahaah I hope she gives you herpes!**

Drake	**Thanks now my mother wants to go get me tested**

Lexi	**BAHA**
Tyrone	**Good thing you only sucked my cack last night**
Drake	**But you got the D in your B**
Imelda	**hahahahahaha**
Tyrone	**I dont remember that...i think you fucked me so hard i blacked out**
Drake	**my weiner is just so big, when you asked me to dickslap you I knocked you out :/**
Tyrone	**Yea im going to the doctor right meow, i think you broke my neck**
David	**Dang haha**
Gina	**HAHAHA**

Lino	**That's why I don't fuck girls at that High School. #Reality**
Simeon	**Wait, I see all these posts about this shit but what happened?**
Lino	**You gave all the girls at town h.s. chlamydia**
Simeon	**Hahahaha iim 90% sure I didn't give it to them haha**
Wyatt	**so many hoez at town h.s. bt sooooooo many of em just dnt keep dey pussy clean an right...smdh fuckin disappointments.. an then dudes fuck em an sexual transmit dat shit tryin to swack swack swack all of em lololol**
Lino	**Hahahahahahahahahah my nigga!**
Dallas	**lol I feel you.**
Ron	**Its funny cause some of the ones that probs have it, even liked it lol!**
Miley	**Idk how I got dragged into this shit but stop saying I have shit wen I definitely don't! I'm so over this!**
Lino	**Do I know you?**
Lino	**.... O_o**
Miley	**Idk but a lot of people have told me your the one saying this so I just wanted to clarify to u and everyone because its really making me upset**
Lino	**I apologize but you have been lied to. I have nothing to do with this rumor. Ask David himself. That's all I have to say.**
Miley	**Ok thanks**
Lino	**No problem**

SLANG & EMOTICONS TRANSLATION

AF	AS F**K	**FER**	FOR
ASAP	AS SOON AS POSSIBLE	**FML**	F**K MY LIFE
AWK	AWKWARD	**FSU**	F**K SHIT UP
AWKAF	AWKWARD AS F**K	**FTW**	F**K THE WORLD
BARS	XANAX	**FUGLY**	F**KING UGLY
BB	BABY	**G**	GANGSTER
BF	BOYFRIEND	**G2G**	GOT TO GO
BFF	BEST FRIENDS FOREVER	**GRIT**	CIGARETTE
BFFL	BEST FRIENDS FOR LIFE	**GTFO**	GET THE F**K OUT
BOO	BOYFRIEND/ GIRLFRIEND	**HAHA**	LAUGHING
BS	BULLSHIT	**HBIC**	HEAD BITCH IN CHARGE
BTDUBS	BY THE WAY	**HMU**	HIT ME UP
BTW	BY THE WAY	**HOLD UP**	WAIT A MINUTE
BUTTHURT	FEELINGS HURT	**HUTCH**	BITCH
CLAP	GONORRHEA (STD)	**IDC**	I DON'T CARE
CLOUD 9	FEELING HIGH	**IDFK**	I DON'T F**KING KNOW
DEF	DEFINITELY	**IDGAF**	I DON'T GIVE A F**K
DGAF	DON'T GIVE A F**K	**IDK**	I DON'T KNOW
DGK	DIRTY GHETTO KIDS	**ILY**	I LOVE YOU
DIP	LEAVING	**IMY**	I MISS YOU
DK	DON'T KNOW	**JK**	JUST KIDDING
DTF	DOWN TO F**K	**KICKS**	SHOES
EWW	DISGUSTED	**LADDERS ALL DAY**	XANAX ALL DAY -
FADED	HIGH, STONED, DRUNK	**LATER**	BYE
FB	FACEBOOK	**LAWL**	LAUGHING

LMAO	LAUGH MY ASS OFF	**SMH**	SHAKE MY HEAD (DISAPPOINTED)
LMFAO	LAUGHING MY F**KING ASS OFF	**SMFH**	SHAKE MY F**KING HEAD
LOL	LAUGHING OUT LOUD	**SMMH**	SHAKE MY MOTHER F**KING HEAD
LSD	D-LYSERGIC ACID DIETHYLAMIDE	**STD**	SEXUALLY TRANSMITTED DISEASE
MAYNE	MAIN FRIEND	**STFU**	SHUT THE F**K UP
MIA	MISSING IN ACTION	**SWAG**	STYLE, COOLNESS, CONFIDENCE
MILF	MOTHER I'D LIKE TO F**K	**TABS**	ACID, LSD
MLIA	MY LIFE IS AWESOME	**TEHE**	GIGGLE
MOFO	MOTHER F**KER	**TEHEE**	GIGGLING
NBD	NO BIG DEAL	**TMI**	TOO MUCH INFO
NTY	NO THANK YOU	**TTYL**	TALK TO YOU LATER
NVM	NEVERMIND	**TXT**	TEXT
OBVI	OBVIOUSLY	**WTF**	WHAT THE F**K
OCN	OF COURSE NOT	**WTH**	WHAT THE HELL
OMFG	OH MY F**KING GOD	**ZANIES**	XANAX
OMG	OH MY GOSH	**n166a**	NIGGA
PERF	PERFECT	**143**	I LOVE YOU
PLANKS	XANAX	**2BH**	TO BE HONEST
PLUR	PEACE LOVE UNITY RESPECT	**4/20**	NATIONAL WEED SMOKING DAY
POPPIN	GOIN ON, HAPPENING	**h3z @ k33pEr d03**	HE'S A KEEPER DOE
PPL	PEOPLE	**>.<**	FRUSTRATED
ROFL	ROLLING ON FLOOR LAUGHING	**</3**	BROKEN HEARTED
SKANK	SLUT OR UNHYGENIC PERSON	**<3**	HEART
SMDH	SHAKING MY DAMN HEAD	**:)**	HAPPY FACE

:(	SAD FACE	*$	STARBUCKS
;(	CRYING FACE	$#!%	SHIT
:/	SARCASM	X_x	DEAD OR IN TROUBLE
#	TWITTER HASH TAG	:L	LAUGHING
*	TYPO	:F	DROOLING
XD	LAUGHING FACE	:J	SMIRK
>3	HATE	:Q	SMOKING
:'(	CRYING	:S	CONFUSED
:')	CRYING WITH JOY	:T	SIDE SMILE
:D	HAPPY	:X	ZIPPED LIPS
:DD	VERY HAPPY	:-)	SMILE, HAPPY
:P	STICKING TONGUE OUT	:-(	SAD
:d	TONGUE FACE	;)	WINK
=)	HAPPY	;-)	WINK
=.=	TIRED	;D	WINK
=0	SHOCKED	;O	JOKING
:O	SURPRISED	;P	WINK & STICKING TONGUE OUT
o.o	SHOCKED	??	WHAT?
^.^	HAPPY	?_?	CONFUSED, LOST
^.~	WINK	<333	MULTIPLE HEARTS
^_^	SATISFIED	>:O	ANGRY
:<	SAD, FROWNING	>O<	YELLING
^5	HIGH FIVE	>_<	FRUSTRATED
//	LOVE, I LOVE YOU	><	FRUSTRATION
(!)	SARCASM	>,<	ANGRY, ANNOYED
$_$	HAS MONEY	>.>	SUSPICIOUS, WARY
%)	DRUNK	>//<	EMBARRASSED, BLUSHING

>3	HATE (OPPOSITE OF <3)	:|	NOT FUNNY, DISAPPROVAL
>:(	ANGRY	=*	KISS
>:)	EVIL GRIN	=/=	NOT EQUAL TO
>:D<	HUG	=3	CUTE/GOOFY FACE
<B	HATE	=D	HAPPY
<3U	LOVE YOU	=F	VAMPIRE
<4	MORE THAN LOVE (<3)	=|	INDIFFERENCE
_	IN LOVE, DAZED	=P	STICKING TONGUE OUT
+_+	DEAD MAN	=S	CONFUSED
-.-	ANNOYANCE	=X	NO COMMENT
-_-	ANNOYED, TIRED	=[	SAD
.-.	SAD, UNHAPPY	=]	HAPPY
:$	EMBARRASSED	}:-)	DEVILISH SMILE
:&	TONGUE TIED, SPEECHLESS	@.@	CONFUSED
:>	MISCHIEVOUS SMILE	@_@	DAZED, HYPNOTIZED
/O/	ARMS IN THE AIR, HAPPY	@@@	WARNING OF PARENTS NEARBY
/O\	FRUSTRATED, HANDS ON HEAD	^^^	REFERING TO LINE ABOVE
:(:)	PIG	vvv	REFERING TO LINE BELOW
:(|)	MONKEY	8====D	PENIS
@}--->---	A ROSE	O_O	SHOCK
:*	KISS	o.O	CONFUSED
:-*	KISS	D:<	ANGRY FACE
:[	SAD, VAMPIRE	("	SIDEWAYS SMILE
:]	HAPPY	X)	MISCHIEVOUS SMILE
:{)	HAPPY WITH A MOUSTACHE		

www.ingramcontent.com/pod-product-compliance
Lightning Source LLC
Chambersburg PA
CBHW071149050326
40689CB00011B/2042